Enrollment Form

☐ *Yes!* I WANT TO BE A *Privileged Woman.*
Enclosed is one *PAGES & PRIVILEGES*™ Proof of
Purchase from any Harlequin or Silhouette book currently for
sale in stores (Proofs of Purchase are found on the back pages
of books) and the store cash register receipt. Please enroll me
in *PAGES & PRIVILEGES*™. Send my Welcome Kit and FREE
Gifts – and activate my FREE benefits – immediately.

More great gifts and benefits to come.

NAME (please print)

ADDRESS   APT. NO

CITY   STATE   ZIP/POSTAL CODE

PROOF OF PURCHASE ONLY

NO CLUB!
NO COMMITMENT!
*Just one purchase brings
you great Free Gifts and
Benefits!*

Please allow 6-8 weeks for delivery. Quantities are limited. We reserve the right to
substitute items. Enroll before October 31, 1995 and receive one full year of benefits.

Name of store where this book was purchased_____

Date of purchase_____

Type of store:
☐ Bookstore   ☐ Supermarket   ☐ Drugstore
☐ Dept. or discount store (e.g. K-Mart or Walmart)
☐ Other (specify)_____

Which Harlequin or Silhouette series do you usually read?

_____

Complete and mail with one Proof of Purchase and store receipt to:
U.S.: *PAGES & PRIVILEGES*™, P.O. Box 1960, Danbury, CT 06813-1960
Canada: *PAGES & PRIVILEGES*™, 49-6A The Donway West, P.O. 813,
North York, ON M3C 2E8

SD-PP5B

▼ DETACH HERE AND MAIL TODAY! ▼

Angel Had Been In Love With Alex Her Whole Life.

Not that she'd ever told him. Him or anyone. But what was even worse than watching him from a distance over the years as he married that stuck-up twit with the finishing school accent and slowly turned into a stuffed shirt, was the fact that Angel had never gotten over him.

She knew about his divorce. She knew about his daughter. She knew that he'd dropped all his old buddies.

And she also knew she was *still* in love with him.

Dear Reader,

Are you looking for books that are fresh, sexy, and wonderfully romantic? Then look no more, because you've got one of them in your hands right now! Silhouette Desire, where man meets woman...and love is the result.

When you enter the world of Silhouette Desire, you travel to places where the hero is passionate...ready to do *anything* to capture the eternal affections of the heroine. He's a guy you can't help but fall a little in love with yourself...just as the heroine does. And the heroine—whether she's a full-time mom or full-time career woman—is someone you can relate to!

And in Silhouette Desire you'll find some of romance fiction's finest writers. This month alone we have Dixie Browning, Lucy Gordon, BJ James, Susan Crosby, Judith McWilliams and Ryanne Corey. And where else, but in Silhouette Desire, will you find the *Man of the Month* or a bold, sensuous new miniseries such as MEN OF THE BLACK WATCH?

Silhouette Desire is simply *the* best in romance...this month and every month! So, enjoy....

Sincerely,

Lucia Macro
Senior Editor

Please address questions and book requests to:
Silhouette Reader Service
U.S.: 3010 Walden Ave., P.O. Box 1325, Buffalo, NY 14269
Canadian: P.O. Box 609, Fort Erie, Ont. L2A 5X3

Dixie Browning

ALEX AND THE ANGEL

SILHOUETTE *Desire*

Published by Silhouette Books

America's Publisher of Contemporary Romance

SILHOUETTE BOOKS

ISBN 0-373-05949-3

ALEX AND THE ANGEL

Copyright © 1995 by Dixie Browning

Books by Dixie Browning

Silhouette Desire

Shadow of Yesterday #68
Image of Love #91
The Hawk and the Honey #111
Late Rising Moon #121
Stormwatch #169
The Tender Barbarian #188
Matchmaker's Moon #212
A Bird in the Hand #234
In the Palm of Her Hand #264
A Winter Woman #324
There Once Was a Lover #337
Fate Takes a Holiday #403
Along Came Jones #427
Thin Ice #474
Beginner's Luck #517
Ships in the Night #541
Twice in a Blue Moon #588
Just Say Yes #637
Not a Marrying Man #678
Gus and the Nice Lady #691
Best Man for the Job #720
Hazards of the Heart #780
Kane's Way #801
Keegan's Hunt #820
Lucy and the Stone #853
Two Hearts, Slightly Used #890
†*Alex and the Angel* #949

Silhouette Books

Silhouette Christmas Stories 1987
"Henry the Ninth"
Spring Fancy 1994
"Grace and the Law"

Silhouette Special Edition

Finders Keepers #50
Reach Out To Cherish #110
Just Deserts #181
Time and Tide #205
By Any Other Name #228
The Security Man #314
Belonging #414

Silhouette Romance

Unreasonable Summer #12
Tumbled Wall #38
Chance Tomorrow #53
Wren of Paradise #73
East of Today #93
Winter Blossom #113
Renegade Player #142
Island on the Hill #164
Logic of the Heart #172
Loving Rescue #191
A Secret Valentine #203
Practical Dreamer #221
Visible Heart #275
Journey to Quiet Waters #292
The Love Thing #305
First Things Last #323
Something for Herself #381
Reluctant Dreamer #460
A Matter of Timing #527
The Homing Instinct #747

*Outer Banks
†Tall, Dark and Handsome

DIXIE BROWNING

has written over fifty books for Silhouette since 1980. She is a charter member of the Romance Writers of America and an award-winning author who has toured extensively for Silhouette Books. She also writes historical romances with her sister under the name Bronwyn Williams.

One

He felt old. Old, dammit, *old!* Where had it all gone—the dreams, the raw, idealistic ambition, the joyous excitement of being a rutting male animal in his prime? The trouble was, a man's prime was over almost before he realized he was in it. After that, it was all downhill.

By the time he left the office, Alex Hightower was hot and tired. Thinking of the woman he'd be seeing in a couple of hours, he tried to drum up a moderate degree of lust. He was only thirty-eight, for God's sake—there had to be a viable hormone somewhere in his six-foot-two, one-hundred-seventy-three-pound carcass!

Think lust, man. Think long, silken limbs, sweet, pouting lips, soft, full breasts. Think tangled sheets, twisting bodies, explosions of passion that leave a man weak and trembling and hungry for a return engagement.

"Think sex, dammit," he muttered, pulling into his driveway. "Forget the damned furniture market!"

He let himself in the front door of the whitewashed brick house he shared with his fourteen-year-old daughter, Sandy, his thoughts focused on a cool shower, a tall drink, and a good excuse that would get him out of his dinner date. He was on his way to securing the first of those when he heard his daughter on the phone.

"—said I couldn't, but he always changes his mind. Oh, sure, I mean, just because Daddy is straight out of the Crustacean period, that doesn't mean—what? Okay. Huh? Oh, sure, don't worry, I can twist him around my little finger."

Feeling an ache in his midsection that was one part irritation, one part indigestion, and three parts love, he passed the half-open door of his daughter's bedroom without calling out a greeting.

Fifteen minutes under a pounding shower did little to ease his tension, nor did the drink he sipped as he got dressed to go out again. Morosely Alex adjusted his gray-striped tie in front of his bureau mirror, wondering if somewhere among the more obscure laws of nature there was one that decreed that fourteen-going-on-twenty-five-year-old daughters and thirty-eight-going-on-a-hundred-year-old fathers couldn't speak the same language.

No wonder he couldn't drum up the strength to do something about his dismal social life. Being a single father sapped all his energies.

"No," he'd said just that morning to her request—more like a demand—to be allowed to go to some camp-out, rock concert affair.

"But Daddy, everyone in the whole wide world is going," Sandy had wailed. "I'll be laughed out of school if I'm the only one whose parent won't let her go—and besides, I promised!"

"And I said no. No is a complete sentence, Alexandra. It requires neither modifiers nor explanations."

"Oh, God, I hate you!" she'd cried, rushing from the breakfast table in tears. Which was a more or less natural state these days.

After that had come the earring thing. Alex would be the first to admit he knew very little about the female of the species—which was quite an admission from a man who'd been sought after by women from the time he turned fifteen. He did know, however, that girls of fourteen had no business wearing half a pound of hardware dangling from one ear. It wasn't even balanced, for Pete's sake!

"But Daddy, *everybody* does it! I'll look naked without my jewelry!"

"A fourteen-year-old girl—"

"Fourteen and a half, which is practically fifteen, and that's almost sixteen, which is old enough to drive and get married and do almost everything! I know three girls my age who're already pregnant!"

He'd aged ten years right then.

"Just because you're too old to remember what it's like to have any fun, that's no reason why I have to live like a five-year-old in a convent."

"I'm not sure, but I don't think they accept five-year-olds in convents, Sandy. Now, go wash your face." She'd been experimenting with makeup lately. "Quickly, please—I'm already late for an appointment."

He'd inspected her face, refrained from further comment on her earrings, one of which was a stud that didn't bear close examination, the other a barbaric arrangement of jangling spare parts that grazed her bony little shoulder.

Was he being too judgmental? She accused him of it on the average of three times a week, but at least she'd stopped calling him a WASP. Now she called him a DWEM, something she'd picked up at school. It meant Dead White European Male. Which was hardly reassuring. Especially the dead part.

From the mirror, Alex's gaze fell to the silver-framed photograph of Sandy on her eleventh birthday. They shared the pale blond hair and the clear gray eyes, but there the resemblance ended. Sandy had inherited Dina's oval face and flawless features instead of his own bony, angular face, his high-bridged nose and aggressive jaw. Thank God. While he'd never had any problem finding women, he had never deluded himself that his looks were the great attraction. Money was a powerful aphrodisiac.

Devil take it, he was running late again! Mrs. Halsey had been late getting here, and then he'd had the usual dustup with Sandy over having a baby-sitter in for the evening whenever he went out. She'd flounced off to her room and turned up what she referred to as her music until he could practically see the prisms on the chandelier in the dining room below jumping off their hooks.

Before heading downstairs, Alex rapped on his daughter's door. "Sandy? I'll be in before midnight." Time for drinks, dinner, a dance or two, the drive back and perhaps a nightcap if he didn't linger over it. "If you need anything, I'll be at the club." Long pause. "With Carol." Silence. If one could call the death throes of a flock of electric guitars plus the collision of two freight trains silence. She knew better than to assault her ears that way, but neither he nor the doctor could convince her. "Sandy? I'll see you in the morning, sweetheart. And by the way... the word is *cretaceous,* not *crustacean.*"

With a defeated sigh, he descended the elegant curving staircase, glanced into the study, where Mrs. Halsey was engrossed in watching a lineup of barechested male cover models on TV. She didn't even look his way. Shrugging, he set off for his dinner date.

Maybe he should ask Carol to have a little talk with Sandy. Maybe she could get through. It might be worth a try.

But was it worth the risk?

Carol English was everything any man could want in a woman. Attractive, intelligent, well-bred, refined. She'd gone to an all-female academy, graduated from an all-female college. Hell, she was female herself. Which meant that at least she spoke the language. So why not give it a shot? Things could hardly get worse than they were now. His daughter was on the verge of disowning him. She kept dropping hints about this group of social do-gooders somewhere or other who encouraged children to divorce their parents.

On the other hand, he'd been suspecting for some time that Carol saw herself as the next Mrs. Alex Hightower, III. He wasn't quite ready to commit himself to that. He'd sent Sandy out shopping with her a couple of times, but if he let things go much further than that, he just might find himself on a steep and slippery slope. He'd be the first to admit that he needed help. He would even admit that his life had been flat for so long that even trouble was a relief... of sorts.

No, it wasn't. Not when that trouble involved his daughter. No way on earth would he ever see her hurt, not as long as he was above ground and breathing.

But *marriage?*

On the other hand, why not? They were compatible enough, he and Carol. It wouldn't be like taking a chance with a stranger. He missed having sex on a more or less regular basis. Thirty laps around the pool could only go so far to make up for it. He also missed the companionship of being married, not that Dina had ever been much of a companion.

Or all that exciting a sexual partner, come to that, but then, he was older now. More settled. Ready to accept the fact that there wasn't a whole lot of joy in everyday life for the average man.

So why not give it a shot? It would be good for Sandy, having a woman in the house besides Mrs. Gilly, the housekeeper, who was more of an institution than a help. He'd known Carol since kindergarten. They had grown up in the same set, belonged to the same clubs, rebelled briefly at about the same time against the establishment before they'd inevitably become a part of it.

Negotiating late traffic on University Drive with unconscious skill, Alex decided he wasn't quite ready yet to give in. Not for the sex or the companionship, both of which he could probably have had anyway, if he'd insisted. Not even for Sandy's sake. Sooner or later, Sandy had to grow up.

Besides, Carol reminded him too much of Dina. His ex-wife. His unlamented ex-wife, now married to some third-rate title in one of those tiny European principalities known for its skiing, its gambling and the whimsical uniforms of its palace guards.

A Trans Am roared past in the right-hand lane, barely making the light. While the Jag purred quietly, waiting for green, Alex thought back again to his college days. Back in those days he'd been bubbling over with the sheer joy of rebelling. Of kicking over the traces. Full of piss and vinegar, as Gus's mother used to say.

Good old Gus. Gus Wydowski. They'd been an invincible team back in the old days—Alex, Gus and Kurt Stryker. High, Wyde and Handsome, they'd been called by some. Tall, dark and handsome by others.

Alex, last of a long line of textile and furniture barons, and an only child, had been spoiled rotten, to the point where he'd even managed to get kicked out of the school endowed by his grandfather, which was no small achievement. His first few weeks in public school had been sheer hell, until a tough kid named Gus Wydowski, son of a diesel mechanic, had come to his defense and taught him a thing or two about fighting. Including the dangers of tucking his thumbs inside his fists before he busted some jerk on the jaw.

Taught him to play high-passing, hard-hitting, tough-as-nails football, too. Both him and Kurt. In high school, they'd been the invincible three. Gus had gone on to earn a college scholarship, and because both Gus and Kurt had enrolled at N.C. State, Alex had broken ranks with three generations of Duke alumni and followed them there.

The old trio. God, how many years had it been? He wished he could put in a call for Gus's tough common sense and Kurt's overgrown sense of responsibility to help him out of the fix he was in right now, but he doubted if either one of them could offer much advice to a man who was being slowly bent out of shape by his own adolescent daughter.

Pulling into the parking lot of Carol's plush garden apartment complex, he lingered a minute before locking the car, remembering the other part of the old threesome.

The tagalong. The pest. The kid sister from hell.

Now there was a trunk full of trouble, he mused. When it came to trouble, Sandy was a nonstarter compared to Angeline Wydowski. A redheaded, freckle-faced peanut, her folks had called her Angel, but everyone else who knew her called her Devil. With just cause!

"H'lo, darling." The door opened silently, and Carol, looking cool and elegant in a three-piece beige silk outfit, leaned forward and brushed a kiss half an inch from his left cheek.

Alex breathed in the familiar scent of hair spray and Chanel. Like the woman, herself, her scent was classic, nonthreatening. "Sorry I'm late," he said. "Baby-sitter got hung up in traffic."

"Oh, Lex, when are you going to get smart and send that poor child off to boarding school? It would be the making of her, I assure you." Carol stepped back to collect her tiny purse, handed Alex her key and waited while he locked her door. "After all, I'm a product of boarding school, and I turned out reasonably well, didn't I?"

She waited for the requisite compliment, which Alex produced with practiced ease. Attractive, intelligent, he reminded himself—well-bred, refined.

And boring. Unfortunately, Carol was about as exciting as stale croissants.

It was three days later when Alex hurried out of his office. If his mind hadn't been racing six blocks ahead, and at the same time trying to come up with a reasonable excuse to lock his daughter away in a safe place for roughly the next forty years, he probably wouldn't have tripped over the pair of size-five combat boots.

"Ma'am, I'm sorry as—"

"Watch it, Hightower!"

"Do I know you?" The woman had been kneeling—actually, she'd been crawling out from under the massive magnolia that overhung the walkway, feet first. Feet and butt first. Feet and coverall-clad, shapely, sweetly rounded butt first.

"Devil?" he said, disbelievingly. "Devil Wydowski? Great Scott, I was thinking about you just the other day, wondering where Gus was now."

Reluctantly Angeline rose to her full five feet two inches, dusted the knees of her coveralls—not even her designer jeans! Wouldn't you just know she would be hot and sweaty and wearing her oldest pair of coveralls the day she finally, actually, came face-to-face with the man who had broken her heart nearly twenty years ago?

"Root bound," she growled, her thin skin glowing like a stoplight.

"He's bound for *where?*"

"Not Gus, the magnolia." God, he was gorgeous! He didn't possess a single perfect feature—unless it was those dark, clear gray eyes that could look right through a woman's skin and see the lust in her heart.

"Angel, I—"

A car slid into a no-parking zone a few yards away, behind a van with a sign that said Perkins Landscaping & Nursery. The passenger side door swung open, a glowering teenager wearing too much eyeshadow and a miniskirt that was barely decent lurched out, and the car pulled away.

Alex swore silently, angry at being put on the defensive again. He'd been on his way to collect her, with every intention of collaring someone in authority and demanding to know how the counselors in what was supposed to be the best school in town dealt with adolescent females who didn't want to be dealt with.

"Sandy, I was on my way to pick you up, if you'd just—"

"Just been patient. Yeah, yeah, I know. I was patient until I got sick to my stomach, okay? So when Mrs. Toad said she'd drop me off at your office, I figured I'd save you the trouble."

"Mrs. Todd," he corrected automatically. "You know I never mind—ah, what's the use? Angel, this is my daughter, Alexandra. Sandy, Miss Wydowski. You've heard me speak of Gus Wydowski?''

"Nope."

"It's Perkins now," Angel said coolly, as if daring him to make something of it.

"Oh. The van?"

"Mine."

So she was married now. Little Angel-Devil Wydowski. What kind of man would take on that challenge, he wondered in slightly distracted amusement. One glance at her small, square hands revealed nothing more than a layer of dirt and a nice set of calluses. No rings. Evidently gardeners didn't wear jewelry while they worked.

"You haven't changed," he murmured, feeling the need to say something. She hadn't, not really. While her hair might have darkened somewhat from the flaming orange he remembered, her wide open smile hadn't changed a bit. It was almost impossible not to smile back, and the last thing Alex felt like doing at the moment was smiling.

Come to think of it, he couldn't remember the last time he *had* felt like smiling. Another thing that seemed to have withered with age was his sense of humor.

"Pleasetameecha," Sandy said, looking curiously from the woman in the pool-table green coveralls to her father and back again. Sandy towered a good eight lanky inches above the diminutive redhead, Alex a full foot. Watching the color fluctuate in Angel's thin skin, Alex felt for no reason at all as if the sun had suddenly come out after a season of rain.

"Yeah. Me, too." Angel upped the wattage of her smile, extended her hand, grimaced and withdrew it. After wiping it on the seat of her pants, she tried again. "Real neat earring. Did you get it at that new place in Chapel Hill?"

"On Franklin Street? Yeah, it's cool, isn't it?"

Alex looked from one to the other as they exchanged information about where to find the coolest, the baddest, and the cheapest good stuff, totally mystified by the inner workings of the female mind.

But then, what else was new?

Angel had just locked up for the night and was looking forward to a long, hot soak, an entire kielbasa pizza with polski wyrobs, onions and feta cheese, all to herself, plus the first of the new books that had come in the mail just that day.

Plain brown wrapper stuff.

Her favorite reading.

Romances.

At thirty-four, Angel had endured a few too many snide looks from size-zilch bookstore clerks half her age, who were barely literate enough to punch the buttons on a cash register, whenever she plopped down her stack of favorite authors on the counter. One look at her utilitarian-style body, her unmanageable hair and her generic-type face, and they figured her only shot at romance had to come from between the covers of a book.

It was nobody's business that she had been in lust twice and actually married for almost a year, all of which had nothing to do with the fact that she'd been in love practically all her life with that blasted Prince

Charming her brother had taken up with the year she'd turned thirteen.

Thirteen-year-old girls don't fall in love?

Ha! This one had.

Not that she'd ever told him. Him or anyone else. But what was even worse than watching him from a distance over the years as he married that stuck-up twit with the finishing school accent and slowly turned into a stuffed shirt, was the fact that throughout the entire course of her own less than illustrious love life, she had never quite managed to get over the jerk.

She knew about his divorce. Not the reason, but the fact that it had happened. She knew about his daughter, and the fact that he had complete custody of her. Around these parts, when a legend like Alex Hightower III even changed barbers, it was fodder for the gossips.

She also knew he'd gradually dropped all his old buddies. Gus hadn't heard from him in ages. Not that she'd come right out and asked—she had too much pride for that—but there were ways of finding out these things.

It was disgusting. It was a blooming disgrace, the way that man affected her metabolism! And it wasn't his precious pedigree she'd fallen for, either. Both the Reillys, her mother's people, and the Wydowskis went all the way back to Adam and Eve. How much farther could a Hightower go?

Nor was it his money. She'd been stiffed by too many in his tax bracket, both waitressing her way through school and more recently, in the landscaping business.

She just wished she could figure it out. Wished even more that she could come up with a cure. Over the years since she'd first been bitten by the Alex-bug, during several minor crushes, including a brief affair with another member of the country club set, who had relieved her of her virginity and then had the gall to laugh when she'd naively expected a commitment from him—even throughout her brief marriage to Cal Perkins—Angel had never quite managed to forget Alex Hightower.

She knew very well—she had always known—that she was beer and he was champagne, and beer suited her just fine, it really did. It was just that she had this crazy addiction. No matter how long she went without a fix, she could never forget what it was she'd been addicted to.

She should have moved to California. Or maybe Australia. Living in the same town, she'd been forced to watch from the sidelines as the years passed. As her own brief marriage to a man who was too handsome to be true—quite literally—had crashed and burned. Watched from a distance, once she'd pushed her own pain into the background, as all the old joy, all the old sweet, wholesome sexiness that had been so much a part of the Alex Hightower she had once known, had slowly withered away.

Oh, yes, she'd seen him, all right. Only he hadn't seen her for the landscape, which she was usually a part of. At least she had been ever since Cal, her too-good-to-be-true husband, had run off with a bar waitress and wrapped his pickup truck around a scalybark hickory south of town.

Which was when she'd become owner, along with the bank, of a small, marginally successful landscape nursery north of town.

Somehow the business survived her early incompetence. Friends had helped. Gus had helped. He'd fenced in the whole area, put in an alarm system, which she usually forgot to set, modernized her tiny office, and then he'd taken a crew and headed for the coast, where he had a contract to build three cottages, leaving her to sink or swim on her own.

Having been born with neither a life raft nor a silver spoon anywhere on her person, Angel had known what she had to do, and she'd set about doing it. The area north of town, where her place was located, was in the process of being rezoned and developed. Less than a month after his father had died, Cal had started talking about selling out the family business and moving to California.

They had never gotten around to it, which was probably a good thing, because after Cal was killed, Angel had desperately needed something solid to hang on to. Even now, seldom a month went past without an inquiry from some real estate agent or developer.

It wasn't the changing zoning that was the threat. Small farms like hers were grandfathered in. But all the developing that was going on, that was another matter. Actually, it was both good and bad. Good business. Bad taxes.

Which made it only sensible that she refocus her meager advertising budget and go after business in the more affluent sections of town, one of which just happened to be the Hope Valley, Forest Hills area.

Was it her fault if that also happened to be the area where Alex's home and office were located? Was it her fault that occasionally she happened to catch a glimpse of him driving by in that well-bred car of his that probably cost more than she grossed in a year?

Actually, it really wasn't her fault. She'd been advised by someone at the bank, acting strictly in an unofficial capacity, that if she wanted to succeed in business, she had to follow the money. And the money was definitely not in her particular neighborhood. At least not enough of it to pay her ever-increasing property taxes.

Which was why, over the years she'd been treated to several glimpses of Alex on horseback, where the bridle trail meandered close to one of the streets she used regularly as a shortcut. Angel's knowledge of riding was strictly limited. She did know, however, that on that big gray monster of a horse, Alex looked nothing at all like the grizzled cowboys she'd seen on "Lonesome Dove." For one thing, she couldn't picture any one of them wearing shining armor and carrying a lance. Alex easily filled the bill.

But then, he always had.

Even in tennis shorts. Back when she'd first met him, she sometimes tagged along to watch him play just so she could admire his legs and his trim behind, which she would have died if anyone had ever caught her doing.

It hadn't taken much in those days to fuel months of daydreams.

Unfortunately, it still didn't. Talk about a case of arrested development!

"Compost," she muttered. Coming out of the fog, she started hacking at the pizza, which was already cold. One of these days she was going to grow up and accept the fact that Cinderellas who wore combat boots never ended up with the charming prince.

Where was he right now? In his plush office, with his plush secretary? Playing tennis at his plush country club? Having supper with that cute-funny-sad daughter of his?

Not this early. Besides, people like the Hightowers didn't eat supper, they dined. And not while they watched the six-o'clock news, either.

She remembered the first time he'd come to their house for supper. She'd been about fifteen—about the same age as his daughter was now. Pop had died just a few months earlier and she and Gus, Mama and Aunt Zee, had moved into Mama's old house with Grandma Reilly.

Grandma had made one of her boiled dinners. Cabbage, corned beef, potatoes and carrots. Angel could've died. She had prayed for roast beef at the very least, pheasant and caviar being too much to hope for. She'd wanted to open up the dining room that no one had used for a hundred years, but Grandma had said if the kitchen was good enough for the cook, it was good enough for the company, and Mama and Aunt Zee had agreed.

So they'd sat around the kitchen table with an electric fan swiveling noisily on top of the refrigerator, and eaten off the dishes that had come from Krogers with coupons. Alex had asked for seconds and then thirds, and cleaned off his plate each time, and once she'd realized that he wasn't just being polite, she had fallen another few miles deeper in love.

Not that he'd ever suspected it. He'd been kind to her in those days, but only in an offhand way, the way Gus was kind to her. Ignoring her, for the most part. Occasionally teasing her absentmindedly, but invariably coming to her defense whenever she got in over her head, which she was very good at. Polish and Irish was an explosive combination, even third generation.

Alex Hightower. Oh, my. To think she had actually talked to him face-to-face again after all these years.

Two

——

The rock concert option settled to his satisfaction— he'd bartered two weeks at a riding camp for a single wild, unsupervised weekend that would have been hard on her eardrums at the very least—Alex had dealt next with an even more ticklish matter.

Boys. Or rather, one boy in particular.

How did a father explain to a daughter who was wavering painfully between childhood and womanhood that just because a boy was considered the choicest guy in the whole school, just because his father had given him a Corvette for his sixteenth birthday, that that was no reason to allow said daughter to go roaring all over creation with said choice guy?

What was it Gus used to call it? The 3-H Club?

Hooch, hormones and horsepower. It had been a threat then. It was no less a threat now, but it damn well wasn't going to threaten *his* daughter. Not if *he* could help it!

It occurred to Alex that what he needed was another trade-off, only what did you trade a fourteen-and-a-half-year-old girl for the sixteen-and-a-half-year-old jerk she thought she was in love with? Bubble gum?

"Daddy, guess who I saw in the park today?" Sandy slammed into the room, her lanky five-feet-ten-inch frame inadequately covered by a leather miniskirt and an angora sweater that only emphasized her lack of curves.

"Elvis?"

She rolled her eyes. "Daa-addy! The plant lady! You know—your old friend?"

Angel. "The plant lady? You mean the woman who reads meters for the power plant?"

"Daa-addy! Ms. Perkins! The woman you introduced me to last week? She had on these real cool coveralls with her name and everything on the back, and she owns her own company and everything. I think that's real cool, don't you?"

"Cool," Alex agreed. Things had been cool when he was a kid. Later on cool had been decidedly uncool. Good had been boss, or neat, or bad, not necessarily in that order. Now they were cool again. Miniskirts were back. He'd even spotted a pair of bell-bottoms last week.

Mark it down to the recycling craze.

"So anyway, I told her about the trees that keep gunking up our pool, and she said she'd come take a look while she was in the neighborhood, only you need to call her first. She won't come unless you do."

Alex unfolded himself from the deep leather chair, a frown gathering as he took in his daughter's words. "You told her *what?*"

"Well, you did say they probably needed pruning back, didn't you? And she does things to trees and all, so I thought..."

So she'd thought she could distract him by dragging a red herring—or in this case, a redheaded herring—across his path, and while he was looking the other way, she could run wild with Kid Corvette.

"No way."

"But Daddy, you *have* to!"

One of the advantages of having dark brows with blond hair was the effectiveness of the scowl. Without even trying, Alex had perfected it to an art. He didn't have to say a word.

"But, Daddy, you'll embarrass me! I gave my word!"

"Your word is your own to give, Sandy, but the grounds are my concern. If I think the trees need pruning, I'll have Mr. Gilly contact the proper people."

The trouble was, they probably did need pruning. This time of year, the kid he hired to clean the pool spent more time raking the leaves out than Phil Gilly spent raking the yard in a season. Only he didn't see any need to call in Angel Wydowski or Perkins, or whatever her name was now.

After Sandy flounced from the room—her favorite form of locomotion these days—he forked a hand through his hair and sank back into the chair where he'd been reading *The Wall Street Journal.* The stock quotations forgotten, he stared at the pattern of sunlight and shadow that danced across the faded Chinese rug.

Angel Wydowski. Trouble in a pint-size package. She used to hang around after games and wait until they'd each hooked up with a girl, and then ask for a ride home. Somehow, when they'd all crammed themselves into Alex's Mustang, she'd usually managed to install herself between him and whatever cheerleader he happened to be dating at the time.

Devil Wydowski. Little Angel. Once she'd found his sweater after he'd left it on the court after a tennis game and taken a cab all the way to his house to return it.

His mother had *not* been amused.

Neither had hers.

Neither had she when he'd tried to reimburse her for the cab fare.

For nearly forty-five minutes, Alex sprawled in his favorite chair in his favorite room in the twelve-room house in which he'd grown up, and thought back to the days of his brief rebellion. In some ways—hell, in all ways—they'd been the happiest days of his life. He'd been alive then, really alive—aware of all the possibilities, of the promise that had sizzled in his bloodstream like newly fermented wine. Every day had been a fresh adventure, every game and every girl a fresh challenge.

Not Angel, of course. Back in those days, she'd had a crush on him, and he'd been flattered as all get out, because Kurt had been right there, too, and Kurt had been every girl's dreamboat.

Dreamboat. Did that term date him, or what?

But, of course, Angel had been off-limits to both of them. She was Gus's sister, and besides, she was just a kid. Still, Alex had always sort of liked her, even when she drove him up a wall. Nor, to be perfectly honest, had he been unaware of her budding attractions. But whatever thoughts he'd had along those lines, he had managed to shove out of his mind. She'd been a kid, after all. His best friend's baby sister. Off-limits.

Levering himself up again, he poured a finger of Chivas and moved to the window, staring out at the scattering of dogwood and maple leaves that patterned the freshly clipped lawn.

September already. Another year slipped past.

Where had the years gone? All the old excitement? There had been a time when every sunrise had been like a big surprise package, all wrapped up in shiny gold foil with a big, floppy satin bow on top.

Somewhere along the way, he must have torn off all the wrappings and ripped open all the boxes, because they weren't there anymore. Whatever had been inside them was gone, too. He couldn't even remember what it had been.

Except for Sandy. His precious, maddening, hair-graying, blood-pressure-raising Alexandra. She was his gift, the most precious thing in his life.

And he *damned* well wasn't about to share her with any card-carrying member of the 3-H Club!

Angel was in the tub when the phone rang. Having finished half a glass of port and just started on chapter seven, where things really began to heat up, she was tempted to let the machine take it. But then, what if it was a job? Some people still didn't take kindly to electronic commands and hung up before the beep.

And face it—she'd been half expecting Alex to call. Sandy had said he would. Either way, whether he wanted her or not, the Alex she remembered would call and let her know. Gentleman's code, and all that.

"Angel? I hope I didn't call at an inconvenient time."

"No, not at all," she panted, dripping frangipani-scented bubbles all over the marble-patterned vinyl. "Alex? Did Sandy put you on the spot? She sort of insisted I should look at some trees on your property, but I told her I wouldn't unless you said so."

"No, that's fine. I mean, they definitely need looking at. The thing is, the pool was built back in the fifties, and I never got around to enclosing it...."

"I know how it is, you keep on putting off things and then when you finally get around to it, you wonder why you didn't do it years ago."

"Right."

Angel shivered in the draft that crept through the open back door. It was warm for September, but cool when one was standing stark, strip, dripping-wet naked in a draft. "Like storm windows. I never get around to putting them up until winter is practically over."

"Yeah. Well, then. I suppose we should set a time."

"A time for what?"

"To, uh—look at the trees?"

"Are you sure? I mean, just because Sandy and I were talking, and she said something about it—I mean, you probably have your own tree people. Or maybe you'd rather ask around? Actually, I'm more of a landscaper and plant salesman than a tree surgeon.''

She was *turning down business?* What was she, sozzled out of her skull on port wine and paperback romance?

"No, you'll do just fine. So maybe you or your husband could come around? Or send somebody. That would be just fine, too. Either way, whenever someone's in the area, my housekeeper can tell him anything he needs to know. Her husband—that's Phil Gilly—he sort of looks after things outdoors.''

"Okay. Fine. Only, first, I don't have a husband anymore, and second, I do all the estimates personally—and I can come anytime it's convenient since I'm doing two places in Hope Valley and there's this citizens committee that's asked me to look at the magnolias outside your office building. Did you know some jerk wants to take them out because they hide his precious architecture? Those trees were there when the place was practically wilderness! Over my dead body will those trees come down! There's probably a historical society somewhere that looks into—''

"Angel?''

"Oh. Sorry. Wait'll I kick my soapbox out of the way.''

Alex sounded as if he were smiling. "You haven't changed a bit, have you?''

"We've already done that routine. And Alex—I really like your daughter. She's special.''

"Yes, she is," he said quietly, and Angel could hear the pride in his voice. They settled on Thursday if it wasn't raining, late in the afternoon. Long after she hung up, Angel could still hear that deep, whiskey-smooth baritone. If he had any idea what even hearing it over the phone could do to a woman's libido, he'd be shocked right down to his patrician toenails!

The week crept past, but eventually Thursday arrived, and thank goodness, there wasn't a cloud in the sky! Angel had to force herself to concentrate on measuring the Lancasters' new patio and platting the placement of a dozen dwarf hollies, three fifteen-foot willow oaks, and an embankment of blue rug juniper.

Her crew had already taken up the balled and burlapped oaks and loaded them onto the truck. The whole thing should be in place, sodding and all, by Sunday, when the Lancasters planned to celebrate with a patio party.

With her mind on hurrying out to Alex's house, she didn't even take time to add up all the overtime, which just went to show that in some respects, she hadn't improved one bit with age.

Sandy was waiting with a pitcher of fresh lemonade. "It's not from a mix, either," she said proudly. "Mrs. Gilly made it up just for us. Hey, if you need to use the john or comb your hair or anything, the bathhouse is over there."

"Thanks, but combing won't help. My mother says it's a curse Granddad Reilly laid on her when she married my pop instead of the nice Irish boy he had all picked out for her. Neither comb nor brush, nor the finest conditioners shall ever unsnarl these tangled locks," she intoned solemnly.

She grinned, and Sandy pointed to her own waterfall-straight hair. "At least yours is interesting. I wanted to have mine cornrowed, but Daddy wouldn't let me. He won't let me do anything." Sighing, she poured two glasses of lemonade that frosted up invitingly, and hooked a lounge chair with her foot, dragging it over. "Sit. You look like you've been working. Hey, it's really neat, owning your own business and all that. How'd you do it?"

It was impossible not to respond to such frank, fresh admiration. And besides, Angel *had* been working hard. She had plodded over every square foot of raw red mud on the Lancaster site, figuring what went where, allowing for root growth and overhang, and then drawing up a plat her guys could follow.

By the time Alex pulled into the driveway, some forty-five minutes earlier than usual, they had covered Angel's widowhood, which she had glossed over in deference to her listener's youth and innocence, touched on the problems of doing business in this age of city, county, state and federal regulations, backed up by the usual bureaucratic alphabet soup of agencies, and moved on to the stupid rules that prevented a woman of nearly fifteen from pursuing her own interests.

Which in Sandy's case, included a boss hunk named Arvid Moncrief who drove a Vette, and becoming either an artist or an airline pilot.

Alex came around the house, having already shed his coat, turned back the cuffs of his white-on-white monogrammed shirt, and loosened his tie, in time to hear Angel saying, "—hooch, hormones and horsepower. My brother used to say any one of the three could cause trouble, but taken together, they were a surefire recipe for disaster. Now, I'm not saying big brothers can't be a royal pain, because they sure as heck can, but I learned the hard way that it pays to listen to mine. Not that I always do.''

"Not that you ever did, to my knowledge." Alex watched the color come and go in her face, watched her struggle to climb out of the low lounge chair, and felt a sharp, hot pull of sexual awareness that took him totally by surprise.

"What do you mean, the hard way? Hi, Dad, we were just having some lemonade before we get to work. Angel's going to show me how to prune a tree so it scars over just right and doesn't get infected. I guess that's why they call 'em tree surgeons, huh? You used to talk about being a doctor, didn't you?''

How could she have known? That had been another lifetime. Before he'd become a father, before he'd met Dina. Before his father had hammered home his responsibility as the sole heir to two generations of furniture makers.

"Sorry you caught me goofing off," Angel said, her smile as fresh and unabashed as ever. "Don't worry, the meter's not running yet." She set her empty glass on the wrought iron table. "So! Shall we get started, Sandy? I can tell you right now, Alex, you're either going to have to waste a couple of those gorgeous Japanese maples or bite the bullet and cover your pool.''

Another thing about her that hadn't changed, Alex thought as she took out a grubby-looking notebook and put on her business face, was those eyes of hers. The color of lapis, with sparkles of gold that glittered when she laughed.

He'd almost forgotten the way she had of wrinkling her nose when she concentrated. He used to tease her about it back in the days when she'd look for any old excuse to hang around, gazing up at him in a way that had made him feel manly and worldly and about seven feet tall.

How would he handle it if she looked at him that way now?

"I suppose you know that maple roots always head for water. They can be a royal pain where you have a septic tank." *He was thinking hero worship and she was talking septic tanks?* "I'm not sure a pool's much safer."

Sandy started humming the theme from *Jaws,* and Alex found himself grinning. Once, maybe twice every few months he found something to smile about, which made it all the crazier, the way the woman affected him, coveralls and combat boots notwithstanding.

They set off for the pool, Sandy and Angel moving on ahead, Alex lingering to empty the lemonade pitcher into the glass Angel had used. He didn't deliberately seek the place where her mouth had touched, but he didn't avoid it, either.

Kid stuff. God, just let him run into an old friend, and he reverted to his childhood!

Following the two females as they sauntered off down the hill, he couldn't help but admire the way the center seam in Angel's bright green coveralls twitched when she walked. She had the kind of build that, according to the medical experts, was the best kind to have for a healthy heart. Pear-shaped. Full hips, small breasts, tiny waist.

Studying that small-scale, pear-shaped body from behind, it occurred to him that it wasn't his own heart that was giving him trouble at the moment, but a part of him that had been anesthetized for so long, he'd damn near forgotten it existed.

He was aroused. By a woman in coveralls and combat boots. A woman who had come to talk to him about trees and septic tanks. Not only was he embarrassed, he felt guilty! Angel Wydowski had definitely grown up, but she was still off-limits. She'd said she was no longer married, so that was no problem, and he was certainly long past the age where he could be led around by his gonads.

But she was still Gus's kid sister. Now that he had a daughter of his own to protect, Alex understood fully why Gus had come down so hard on any guy who'd even looked at his kid sister for more than five seconds running.

The old 3-H Club. Kid stuff. This time, there was no hooch involved, only watered-down lemonade. Definitely no horsepower. What could be safer than a stroll across a backyard, with a daughter acting as chaperon? The only trouble was, a few hormones he'd thought had gone into early retirement were evidently still alive and kicking.

His stride took on elements of swagger, his grin a certain macho quality that would have sent him gunning for any kid who came sniffing around his daughter with the same look on his face. By the time he caught up with them, they were designating which branches above what height would have to go. Every time Angel lifted her arm to gesture, Alex found himself unconsciously searching her chest for any indication that she'd matured in the bosom department. Why couldn't she wear jeans and a T-shirt like everyone else?

Judas Priest! When had he turned into a dirty old man?

Embarrassed at the direction his thoughts had taken, he stared at the spreading limbs and tried to concentrate on what she was saying. Something about how close to the trunk to make the cut so that it would scar over properly.

Before he could come up with a single intelligent question that would prove he was interested in her mind and not lusting after her body, the phone inside the house began to ring. Reprieved, he turned toward the house just as Mrs. Gilly stuck her head out the French doors. "Sandy, it's for you. Your young man."

Alex's knees locked. His angular features took on a steely look that had made more than one young man swallow his Adam's apple. "If that's Moncrief, Alexandra, you can tell him—"

But Sandy was already gone, long legs flashing in the late afternoon, early autumn sunlight.

Angel came up silently beside him. "Not that it's any of my business," she said quietly, "but if Sandy were my daughter—"

"She's not." He regretted his short reply even before he saw the gold flecks in her eyes disappear, leaving them opaque. "Sorry. Nothing personal, Angel, but Sandy's my problem."

He might have known she wouldn't back down. "Fine. But I hope you know how lucky you are to have such a problem. She's a bright girl, Alex, but even the smartest girl needs more than some fathers are willing to give."

"Are you offering your services?" Another dig he regretted too late. The trouble was, since his divorce he'd had to go on the defensive where women were concerned.

"To Sandy, maybe—if she needs me. Not to you." Very deliberately, she scribbled a name and number on a scrap of paper, tore it off and then closed her notebook, twisted her mechanical pencil and tucked them both away in the pocket of her coveralls. With a smile that was about as genuine as a ten-dollar Rolex, she said, "Here's the name and number of the best tree guy in town. He's not cheap, but your trees will be in good hands. I'll see you around, okay?"

Alex jammed the scrap of paper into his shirt pocket without even glancing at it. "Angel, wait! Look, I'm sorry, okay? I didn't mean that the way it sounded, it's just that—"

"I'll tell Gus I saw you, shall I? He usually calls on weekends."

Feeling lower than pond scum, Alex watched her walk away, her short legs twitching the heavy cotton twill enticingly over her rounded buttocks. He cursed himself for being rude, for being an arrogant jerk. And then, as he watched her tug open the door of her van and swing herself up by the side view mirror, he cursed himself for being a lecherous bastard.

Watching her back down the driveway, he wondered if she still had to sit on a pillow, the way she had when he and Gus had taught her to drive Gus's old Falcon. She'd begged to try out Alex's Mustang, but Gus had put his foot down. Alex would probably have given in. He'd had a secret weakness for Gus's kid sister in those days. Part of being an only child, he'd tried to tell himself.

"Hey, where's Angel going?" Sandy asked plaintively, coming to stand beside him at the edge of the driveway.

"Home, I suppose. It's getting late."

"But I wanted to invite her to have dinner with us tonight. Mrs. Gilly said it would be all right."

"Mrs. Gilly doesn't make the rules around here, in case it escaped your notice."

"Is it because she's wearing, like, coveralls? Daddy, that's just plain arctic! Nobody—"

"Archaic," he corrected automatically.

"I mean, nobody cares about junk like that anymore! I think your old rules stink!"

"I'm sure you do, but as long as you're—"

"I know, I know—as long as I'm living under your roof, I have to bow and scrape to your royal highness."

A grin threatened to kick in again, against all logic. He had a pretty fair notion what she was thinking, and it wasn't about his royal highness. "Sorry, sweetheart, it's the system. It suckers us all in, and before we know it, we're nothing but mind-numbed robots, having to wash up before meals, having to listen to DWEM composers instead of demolition derbies set to music while we dine. Having to—"

"All right, all right!" Out came the lower lip. Down came the scowling brows. "But I'm not going to stop being friends with her, I don't care what you say! And I might even work at her place next summer. She hires, like, school kids sometimes."

"Fine with me," he said mildly. Last week it was the record shop at the mall. The week before that, she was planning to look for a job at a riding stable. At least she'd given up on the airline thing. "By the way, I won't be in for dinner tonight, but I won't be out late, either, if you want to talk after you finish your homework."

She looked hurt. He didn't want to see it. "If I want to talk, I'll call Angel. At least she treats me like an adult, which is more than I can say about *some* people."

Pond scum. That about said it all.

Before they even ordered dinner, Alex knew the evening was going to be a bummer. Carol had made several pointed remarks about friends whose daughters went off to school and how well it turned out for all concerned.

"I'd be the first to admit I lose patience sometimes—whoever said raising a daughter alone was easy, obviously never had tried it—but I'd miss her too much, Carol. She's all I've got left." He attempted a smile, but it failed for lack of conviction. "I guess it comes of being an only child of an only child. We only children have special obligations. We have to be there for each other, whether or not it's always convenient."

"Nonsense! Darling, Sandy has plenty of friends. No girl her age wants a father always hanging around, cramping her style."

"Maybe her style needs a bit of cramping."

"And maybe she just needs to be with kids her own age. It's not as though you're some doddering old relict, gathering his family around him for support in his waning years. You're young, healthy, virile—and certainly more than able to take on additional responsibility."

"Additional responsibility?"

"You could even have a second family."

"Not if I want to stay sane."

"That's what boarding schools are for. Did it ever occur to you, darling, that Sandy would adore having a baby sister or brother? It would give her something to do with her evenings besides hanging around boys."

A waiter appeared at his side, and Alex ordered the broiled chicken for Carol and braised calf's liver for himself. Maybe he needed more iron in his diet. God knows, he needed something he wasn't getting.

"Things are different now than when we were kids, Carol. These days, girls Sandy's age are exposed to a lot of new dangers. I want her to know—especially after Dina—" He shrugged. "At any rate, she needs to know she comes first with me. I'm not sure taking on a second family would be the thing to do."

"Oh, but the experts all say—"

"Any dozen experts will say at least a dozen different things. Experts are like statistics. You can always find a few to back most any crackbrained theory you want to propose. The trouble comes when you put theory to the test and find out it's full of holes. I guess I'll just have to blunder along the best way I can and hope for the best." Leaning back, he crossed his arms casually over his chest, hoping she would take the hint.

Subject closed.

"Now . . . shall I order us another bottle of wine?"

Later that evening, Alex told himself that he owed Angel a call. Owed her an apology, too, only he wasn't entirely sure which offense to apologize for first. Cutting off her attempt to help with Sandy, or lusting after her delectable little body.

The truth was, he suspected it was more than her body he lusted after. She made him smile. She made him want to laugh. She made him feel young again.

Which was why he decided not to call her. Not to expose himself to danger. He had enough to deal with without waking any sleeping dragons.

Three

———

Having recently studied every new line, every slightest hint of aging on Alex's face, Angel now examined her brother with the same squinty-eyed concentration. "Ah-*ha!* Six more gray hairs," she pronounced with grim satisfaction. Why was it that men improved with age, while women only aged?

While he would never be called classically handsome, with his wicked blue eyes and his full black beard, Gus looked like the pirate hero on the cover of one of her new paperback romances. He had aged remarkably well.

So had Alex, dammit.

There was a lot to be said for aristocratic bone structure, she concluded dismally. So far as the naked eye could discern, she didn't even *possess* any bone structure.

"What happened, did you fall on your head?" She indicated a scar that snaked into the edge of his unruly hair, diagonally up from the one she happened to know was hidden by his beard.

"Two-by-four. Guy didn't signal his turn in time. Hey, Angel, what's with the blinking lights? Does that happen often?"

"No more than once or twice a week. Want a bagel with your coffee?"

"Hmm. I should've checked out the wiring last time I was here. A bagel? Yeah, sure, hon. Remind me to get my meter out of the truck when I bring in my bag, will you?"

Angel poured coffee, set out a crock of cheese and a half-dozen fresh bagels. She'd been working like a Trojan all day. Gus had pulled in just before dark, looking gaunt and tired, but when she'd offered to cook him a meal, he'd said he wasn't hungry.

The day Gus Wydowski wasn't hungry was the day they laid him out in the front parlor with a lily in his fist. Something was bothering him, and it was her duty as his only relative east of the Mississippi to drag it out of him.

She decided on the indirect route. She wasn't very good at it, but one didn't butt heads with Gus Wydowski and come out the winner. "Guess who I saw twice last week?" she mentioned casually as she slathered cheese on half a bagel and handed it across the table. "Hightower. And I met his daughter, too, and she's something else. Blond, gray eyed, tall—she looks like Dina, but she's a lot more interesting, even at fourteen."

Gus had been in love with Dina. They'd never spoken of it, and Angel didn't think Alex had ever guessed, but she'd known practically from the first. If she hadn't already hated the woman for stealing Alex, she would have hated her for that. Dina ex-Hightower was a gold-plated bitch, even if she was a countess or duchess or whatever in some two-bit kingdom nobody'd ever heard of.

Poor Gus, he'd stood up with Alex at the wedding, and then headed for the hills, seven months short of graduation. He never had gone back for his degree.

"Great. So how's Alex?" Without waiting for an answer, he continued. "You know, I've got a job lined up at the beach, kid. Probably take until November to get it under cover. Why not take a break and come on down for a week or so?"

"Aren't you even curious?"

Gus reached for another bagel, smeared it with cheese and then got up and rummaged around in her refrigerator for something sweet to spread on top of that. "Curious?"

"About Alex. How he's doing and all. You two haven't seen each other in years, and you used to be close as two nuts in a hull. Make that three, counting Kurt."

"So? I've been busy. Have you got any lime marmalade?"

She took a jar out of the pantry, opened it and handed it over. "Your teeth are going to rot out. You know, if Alex were my best friend, and I hadn't seen him in—"

"All right, already! Lay off, will you?"

"Dina's history, Gus. I doubt if Sandy even remembers much about her. Sandy's their daughter, did I tell you? She's about the same age now that I was when—"

"Yeah, I know. The same age you were when you embarrassed the hell out of me by coming on to Alex."

Angel slammed her cheesy knife down onto the yellow enameled table. "I did not! I never in my life came on to any man—at least, not to Alex!"

Gus grinned, and even his sister was forced to admit that the years had not diminished his old appeal. He and Alex were as different as day and night—yet no woman alive could fail to appreciate either one of them. Singly or together, they were enough to drive a woman up a wall.

Gus piled on marmalade with the skill and precision of a master craftsman. "So... you've still got a thing for old Lex, huh?"

"Sure, like I still have a thing for poison ivy."

"Why not just scratch and be done with it?"

"What, the poison ivy?"

"No, witchlette—Alex. He's free. You're free. Why not give it a go? The worst that could happen would be that he'd turn you down and you could finally mark him off your wish list."

"You mean the *best* that could happen! The worst would be if he took one look and started laughing like a hyena." Angel flung herself up from the table and stalked over to the kitchen sink just as the lights blinked again. "Fine brother you turned out to be," she grumbled. "For your information, Alex's seeing this woman named Carol Something-or-other. You probably knew her—she's part of that country club set. Anyway, poor Sandy's scared out of her gourd he's going to marry her. She says this Carol person keeps sending her information about boarding schools and dropping heavy hints about how much fun it is to live in a dorm with girls her own age and date boys from all the best prep schools."

"For a kid you just met, you two sure got down to cases in a hurry."

Angel shrugged. "So we happened to hit it off. Maybe because Sandy knows I'm no threat to her in that respect. She did say, though, that the day Alex marries this Carol person is the day she's out of there." She ran a sink full of sudsy water and plopped in her breakfast dishes, her lunch dishes, and the accumulation from last night's snacks. "I don't think she's planning on moving into the palace with Dina, either. There's this boy she knows who drives a Vette? From her description, my guess is he's a perfect candidate for your old 3-H Club."

Gus grinned, his teeth startlingly white in his dark, bearded face. "Oh-oh. Maybe I'd better give Hightower a call and offer him a little moral support."

"I think you should. Gus...what's worrying you?" So much for the subtle approach.

He slanted her a wary look. "Nothing's worrying me, kid. I've got more business than I can handle, but I can handle that."

Angel knew a stone wall when she ran into one. He'd tell her in his own sweet time. *If* he told her at all. Gus was a very private man. "You're not fooling me, you know. You've got that squinty look around your eyes you used to get when you were worried about a game or a test or Daddy's finding out you'd been drinking.''

His eyes were the same color as her own, only hers were several shades darker. "Just remember, I'm always here if you want to talk."

Passing by on his way to the telephone, Gus grabbed her in a bear hug, lifting her off the floor. "Know something, witchlette? You turned out pretty good for a smart-mouthed kid who took to trouble like a duck takes to water."

Alex had just finished filling Sandy in on Gus Wydowski when the door chimes sounded. He'd been advised by his CEO, who had two kids in college and another one in high school, that treating them as adults sometimes produced surprising results. He figured it was worth a try.

Expecting Gus, he swung open the door and found Carol. She was holding out a bouquet of pink roses in one hand and a bottle of his favorite wine in the other.

"Surprise," she crowed softly, leaning forward to kiss the air beside his cheek. "Well, aren't you going to invite me in, darling?"

"Sure, come on in. Uh—did I slip up and forget something?" Alex closed the front door, mentally flipping through his engagement calendar. It was going on eight, and he could have sworn they hadn't made a date for tonight, but he'd had a lot on his mind lately.

"I've been in Raleigh all day—did I tell you I'm sitting for my portrait? That's where the roses came from—I'm holding them in my pose, wearing white silk brocade with Mother's sable cape over one shoulder. Anyway, I thought as long as I was passing so close, I'd stop in and see if you wanted to go to the club dance next weekend. Oh, hi, Sandy. Are we all finished with our homework?''

''I'm all done with mine, but I guess you're still working on yours, huh?'' Her voice held that note of sugary innocence Alex had come to know all too well in the past few months. He shot her a warning glare, but before he could suggest an early evening, the chimes sounded again.

This time, it was Sandy who flung open the door. ''Oh, hi, you must be Mr. Wydowski, Daddy said you were on your way over. Angel, are you sure he's your brother? I mean, like, you guys don't look the least bit alike. Come on in, we were expecting you.''

Alex had been expecting Gus. In his new adult-to-adult mode, he'd suggested that Sandy might care to play hostess for a few minutes before going upstairs to watch TV until bedtime.

Gus hadn't said anything about bringing his sister along. Not that she wasn't welcome, but dammit, there it was again—the same crazy reaction he'd felt when he'd first spotted her crawling, butt-and-boot-soles first, out from under the magnolia tree. He *never* reacted to women this way!

At least, not in the past twenty-odd years. ''Gus...Angel,'' he murmured, trying not to stare at her purple-figured slacks and turtleneck sweater. God, she lit up a room!

Carol, a study in shades of beige, lifted a flawlessly penciled brow. ''Friends of yours?'' she said under cover of Sandy's effusive chattering.

"Angel and Gus Wydowski—Angel Perkins now. We go way back."

With a smile that could have been cast in porcelain, Carol said, "How lovely. I'd forgotten that you attended public school for a few years." She summed up and dismissed Angel and, without missing a beat, turned to Gus, her eyes widening ever so slightly. "I'm Carol, of course. Carol English. I'm sure Alex must have mentioned me."

Doing his best to ignore Sandy and Angel, who were headed for the study, arm in arm, Alex allowed himself a moment to appreciate Gus's reaction to Carol and vice versa. Whatever his appeal was to women, Gus hadn't lost it. Baggy khakis and a flannel shirt that had seen better days did little to disguise his muscular build. The girls used to fall all over him—those that weren't swarming around Kurt. Or himself, Alex thought modestly.

If Gus had had a thing for Dina—and he had, although Alex wasn't supposed to know about it—he ought to go for Carol in a big way. Same blond hair in a well-groomed pageboy style. Same impeccable, understated sense of fashion.

He had a sudden vision of Carol wearing something like Angel's purple print pants, or her pool-table green coveralls with Perkins Landscaping scrolled across the back in acid yellow. She'd be totally eclipsed.

Grinning, he led the way into the study.

The talk was general for the first few minutes until Carol began conducting a well-bred inquisition with Gus as her victim, casting the occasional oblique look at Alex.

He knew his role. He'd played it too many times with Dina during their brief marriage, but tonight he was just too damned tired to play the jealous husband.

So he leaned back in his chair—or rather, the smaller of the two leather chairs that had been a prototype for one of Hightower, Inc.'s older lines. Angel had homed in on the one he habitually used, slipping off her shoes and tucking her feet up beside her.

She was wearing pink wool socks. For some reason, that got to him.

As the currents of conversation eddied around the small group, Sandy dragged a footstool over to Angel's chair, leaving Carol enthroned in a tapestry-covered Queen Anne wing chair.

Feeling oddly restless, Alex rose. "What'll it be, Gus, the same old bourbon and branch?"

"Nothing for me, thanks. I'm driving. I don't want to give the witchlette an excuse to take over my new wheels." He turned away from Carol, grinning at the other three. "She ever tell you about the time I had to bail her out of the tank for trying to outrun a platoon of smokies over on 15-501?"

"Don't listen to him, Sandy, it wasn't at all the way he makes it sound," Angel muttered. "My accelerator got stuck and I just happened to cream a few road signs while I was trying to work it loose with my foot."

Grinning—she'd always had the damnedest effect on him—Alex poured wine for the women, grenadine and ginger ale for Sandy, and turned to Gus again. "Why not stay here while you're in town so we can do some serious catching up? We've got plenty of rattling-around room, haven't we, princess?" He called on Sandy to second the invitation, and she beamed at him, making him feel that for once he had done something right.

"Thanks, but I'm all set out at Angel's place. The roof hardly leaks at all in clear weather, and now that she's got the squirrels in her attic under control—" Gus chuckled as his sister tossed a pillow at him. She reminded him that he'd promised to look at her wiring. "Noblesse oblige, Wydowski style. I do her house repairs—she does my mending and feeds me Polish-style pizza whenever I pass through town."

Carol examined her manicure. Sandy immediately wanted to know how to make Polish-style pizza, and the men discussed antiquated wiring and new building codes. The talk moved on to the construction business in general, which happened to be in the middle of an upswing, and the furniture-making business, including Hightower Fine Furniture, Inc., of which Alex was chairman of the board. Gradually the women fell silent as the men talked NAFTA and GATT and the upcoming international fall furniture market in nearby High Point.

Ignored, Carol began to beat a silent tattoo on the arms of her chair with her pale pink fingernails. Sandy gazed openly and admiringly at her father's best friend. Angel's head slid sideways and her eyes finally closed and stayed that way. She'd been up since five, and had put in her usual twelve-hour day before Gus had shown up.

Rising silently, Sandy disappeared, and some twenty minutes later, reappeared, precariously balancing a loaded tray. "Coffee," she called out softly, grinning at the small woman in purple paisley pants who was sound asleep in Alex's leather chair, one bronze-colored curl stirring gently to the rhythm of her breathing.

It was Gus who hurried to relieve her. Giving her the benefit of his lady-killing grin, he took the tray just as it began to tilt. "Did anyone ever tell you you're even prettier than your mama?"

"No sir, but if you'd like to, feel free." She grinned right back, fresh as a chipping sparrow.

"Lex, this kid of yours is trouble on the half shell, I hope you realize it, old man."

"Where do you think all this gray hair came from? Thanks, princess. Now, don't you think—" He'd been about to suggest it was time she turned in, but one scowl from Angel, who had woken up at the scent of fresh coffee, steered him from the brink of disaster. "Uh . . . you'd better sit over here to pour?"

It was past midnight when Gus and Angel left. By that time, Sandy had a new hero and Alex had a new headache. Instead of worrying about a kid in a Vette, he was worrying about a middle-aged guy in a pickup truck.

On the plus side, she hadn't burst into tears and slammed into her room in more than a day and a half now. Things were definitely looking up.

Half-asleep in the plush comfort of Gus's new stretch-cab pickup, Angel thought about Alex's predatory blonde and smiled. It was not a particularly nice smile. By the time the impromptu gathering had broken up, Ms. English had been mad enough to chew nails. "Did you like her?" she murmured against the melancholy strains of "Moonlight In Montgomery" on the CD player.

"Who?"

"Never mind." She wondered absently if Alex still liked boiled dinners.

Gus started swearing when the second fire truck raced past them only a couple of miles from the turn-off to the farm. With a feeling of growing unease, Angel unsnapped her seat belt and leaned forward, watching to see where it went. *Not my road, not my road—please, God, not my road!*

And then she swore, too. Gus downshifted and turned off the pavement onto the graveled road. The instant the pickup skidded to a halt just inside the gate, Angel flung open the door and hit the ground running.

By then it was all over but the smoke. All over but the mess. Wisps of steamy smoke rose from the house, and there was an assortment of fire trucks scattered over what had once been her freshly graveled, beautifully landscaped parking area.

"Lotta smoke damage. Some water, too, I guess. Sorry, lady, but it looks like you're gonna need a new roof. Coulda been a lot worse, though. Kid passing by happened to see the glow through the upstairs windows an' called it in."

Distracted, Angel thanked the volunteer firemen who had responded so quickly to the call and the second crew that had just arrived as backup. She hurried across the rutted ground toward the front door, completely unaware that she was whispering a steady chorus of denial under her breath. "Oh, no—oh, no, no, no."

"Whoa, lady, you don't wanna go inside yet."

She jerked her arm from his grasp. "It's my home, dammit! I'm going inside!"

"Sorry. I can't let you in, ma'am. Smoke's still thick enough to choke a hog. Bound to be some structural damage. A couple of us are going to stick around, make sure it don't flare up again. You got anywheres else you can sleep tonight?"

"I have no intention of sleeping anywhere else. Everything in the world I own is in that house." Again she shook off the restraining hand. "Gus," she wailed, "make him let me go, he won't listen to me!"

"I'll check out the house while you see to the rest of the place."

"Oh, God, my greenhouse," she gasped. Staring dazedly around, she tried to take it all in, but with the flashing lights and a hoard of space aliens in face masks swarming over her territory, nothing seemed real.

"Take a deep breath," Gus said quietly. "The greenhouse looks okay to me. Your shed's still there. The trucks are fine, too."

Fortunately, her van and the old stake-back delivery truck were parked on the far side of the greenhouse, away from the house. A pale sliver of moon gleamed down on the dusty top of her greenhouse and glinted dully off the wet metal roof of her storage shed. "My plants—" she whispered, but the rows of Bradford pears, weeping cherry and ornamental plums stood silently reassuring.

Still, she trudged across the wet gravel, intent on seeing for herself. By the time she had checked the greenhouse, the shed and her two vehicles, some of the throat-clutching panic that had gripped her at first had begun to ease.

"Hey, it's okay, honey," Gus rumbled, coming up silently behind her to gather her in his arms. "It's nothing we can't fix. I'll call in a couple of my guys first thing in the morning and we'll have you back in business in a week's time, I promise."

"Just tell those fire people that I have to get inside," she demanded from the safe haven of her brother's comforting arms. "I *have* to! My checkbook—my toothbrush—oh, Gus, all my albums!"

Angel had been a voracious photographer in her youth, with albums devoted to family, others to friends, and one whole album that nobody knew about devoted entirely to Alex Hightower. She would *die* if anyone found out!

"Easy now, witchlette, it could've been a hell of a lot worse."

She pulled free of his arms, her wide navy blue eyes gleaming up at him through a soot-streaked face. "I know, I know—I'm being silly. Thank God you were here. Look, we can dash inside and grab some blankets and pillows and settle down in the greenhouse for tonight. There's a bathroom of sorts off the office, and—"

"Shh, I've already made arrangements, hon. I'll stick around here until morning—can't do anything until then, anyway, but as soon as it's light enough, I'll check everything out, call in a couple of the guys and start working up a supplies list. By noon I should have a pretty good idea of when you can come home again.''

"Come *home* again!" She wrenched free of his arms and glared up at him. "If you think I'm going to a motel, you're cockeyed crazy! I told you, I'm sleeping in the greenhouse!"

"Yeah, sure you are," he jeered softly. "Along with the mice that come in to eat the seeds, and the snakes that come in to eat the mice, and the—"

"Stop it! Just stop it! I'll sleep in your truck, then."

"What, and leave me to sleep with the mice and snakes? Anyhow, here comes Alex now. Sandy can lend you something to sleep in, and I would be surprised if she couldn't come up with a spare toothbrush." At her fresh wail of anguish, he knuckled her cheek the same way he used to do when, as a child, she'd stumbled into trouble over her head.

"Shh, it'll be okay, small stuff. Trust me. What are big brothers for?"

Stepping away from the shelter of his arms again, Angel sniffed, blinked and smeared her filthy face on her sleeve. "Alex's not my big brother, dammit, you are!"

"I know," Gus said softly, turning to greet the man who came loping across the ruined grounds. "Thanks, Lex. I owe you one."

"God," Alex whispered softly, staring at the smoke-blackened ruins of the once neat little frame house.

"And I owe *you* one, Augustus Timothy Wydowski! Don't think I'll forget it!" Switching her glare to Alex, immaculate in his light gray tweeds and well-bred cotton sweater, she snapped, "I want it on record that I'm going only under duress."

Alex smiled, but it faded almost immediately. Tucking her arm under his, he steered her over the ruts made by the fleet of heavy fire trucks. "Duly recorded, ma'am."

Four

———

Who would ever have thought that the smell of bacon and shaving soap, coffee and toothpaste, could elicit a full-blown fantasy? There was something dangerously intimate about sharing eggs and toast in the small, sunny breakfast room. Alex's silvery gray eyes still had that slightly unfocused look, despite the fact that he was freshly shaved, his hair still damp from the shower.

Half amused, half irritated at her own weakness, Angel wondered when he had last had his eyes examined. Who reminded him of things like that? His secretary? Even Gus, as capable as he was in most ways, had to be reminded to schedule physicals and dental checkups and the occasional eye exam.

Dinner wasn't quite so bad. At least she'd had the day to build up her defenses. And four was a much safer number than two.

At the moment, they were all seated around the oval table in the formal dining room, Alex at the head, Sandy at the foot, with Gus and Angel in the middle. Remembering her grandmother's old enameled kitchen table where once she had entertained a younger Alex over a boiled dinner, Angel could have wept.

Was the table still there? Gus refused to allow her inside the house until he declared it structurally safe. She'd had to content herself with peeping through the windows, most of which were still blackened with smoke, a few of which were broken.

They'd squabbled over it ever since the fire. Finally, just before Gus arrived for dinner tonight, Alex had spoken out. "You've made it perfectly clear that you hate having to accept my hospitality," he'd said. Which was true, only not for the reasons he thought. "You're making things pretty uncomfortable for Gus. He's only thinking of your safety, you know. Poor guy, he feels guilty enough without your constant nagging."

"I've never nagged in my life! And why on earth should Gus feel guilty? He certainly didn't set the fire."

"Possibly because he knew the wiring was old and he didn't do anything about it."

"But he was planning to. Besides, it's my house—it's my responsibility to see that it's safe. Gus is my brother, not my keeper."

Alex hadn't said another word. He didn't have to. Some people were born with the ability to quell a riot with no more than the lift of an eyebrow.

While others, she fumed as she attacked her tiny serving of French vanilla ice cream, still smarting from the set-down he'd administered, could spend a lifetime beating their heads on the same old stone wall without ever learning a blessed thing!

Only it wasn't her head that was aching, Angel thought as she rose and followed the others into the study. At least this time she didn't make the mistake of stacking her dishes and taking them out to the kitchen.

It had been Sandy who had clued her in. "Mrs. G. does that," she'd whispered.

"But I don't mind at all. It's the least I can do, and Mrs. Gilly looks, um ... tired." She didn't want to come right out and say it, but the poor woman looked as if she were long overdue a comfortable retirement. It wasn't as though the Hightowers couldn't afford to put her out to pasture.

"Oh, she's not tired. I mean, she doesn't do all that much anymore, but Daddy says she's got too much pride or something, so we let her do the easy stuff and have a cook and a daily in for everything else. Mrs. G. bosses them around a lot, but Daddy pays real good, and besides, Mrs. G. really does know a bunch of stuff about keeping house, so it works out okay."

Grudgingly Angel gave Alex credit for a quarter of an ounce of sensitivity. At least toward his housekeeper. Pity he couldn't spare a bit for his daughter. But then, as a single father dealing with a headstrong teenage daughter, he was probably doing the best he could.

They had already had words on the subject of Sandy's clothes. Not that it was any of her business. Unfortunately, Angel was constitutionally incapable of minding her own business where her friends were concerned. She called it being helpful. Gus called it being bossy.

And anyway, Sandy's skirts were not really all that short, they only looked that way because at five foot ten, she was mostly legs. And granted, she was a bit heavy-handed with the eyeshadow, but she'd been easy enough to convince when Angel had shown her how much more flattering a light dusting of pale gray was compared to metallic blue.

As for the way she hung on to Gus's every word, and the way her eyes had bugged out when she'd seen him coming from the pool with Alex late last night, that would pass. He was a novelty, that was all. And face it—her brother might not be precisely handsome, but he'd never had any trouble attracting women.

Angel and Sandy had been having a last glass of milk before heading upstairs to bed when the two men had climbed out of the pool and come directly into the house through the side door instead of showering and changing in the bathhouse. Angel had heard Sandy's soft "Oh, wow" as Gus stepped into the kitchen.

Personally, Angel hadn't spared her brother a second glance. She'd been too busy taking in the splendid sight of Alex's tall, rangy body clad only in racing trunks and a towel, the surprisingly dark body hair that formed a tee across his chest and down his abdomen still gleaming with moisture.

There ought to be a law against spandex.

All the same, for Sandy's sake, the sooner Gus left town, the better. Out of sight, out of mind.

Oh, sure, Wydowski! Just like you forgot all about Alex the minute he married Dina and quit hanging out with Kurt and Gus!

Dammit, she didn't need this. She was stressed out enough from dealing with insurance adjusters, answering carpenters' questions and putting off clients, without the added burden of sharing a house with Hightower.

Talk about your inadequate wiring—when a woman was wired for one-ten, she had no business fooling around with two-twenty. What was it about the man? His nose was too big, his jaw was too square—his cheekbones had obviously been chiseled out of raw granite. He was taller than any man needed to be, and to top it off, he was a blasted business executive!

None of the heroes in her favorite romances were desk people. They were cowboys—or test pilots—or maybe secret agents. Men on the run from a devastating hidden past.

Alex Carruthers Hightower the third was a blooming plutocrat. A furniture tycoon. Whoever heard of a hero who made furniture?

Right. He was dull. So how come she had spent the past twenty years of her life following *his* life the way a heliotrope follows the sun?

On Saturday, Sandy insisted on skipping tennis practice and going to work with her. "Tennis is boring. I always do tennis on Saturdays.'' She sighed. She had sighed so much since Gus had left town the night before, promising to return by the middle of the week, that Angel was tempted to warn her against hyperventilation.

Perhaps a bit of distraction was in order. ''Sure, but tell your father first,'' she said.

They were in the upstairs hallway. ''Daddy, I'm going to the shop with Angel,'' Sandy screeched over the banisters.

Alex appeared with a newspaper in hand in the hallway below. His hair was ruffled, the sleeves of his band-necked denim shirt turned back, and a pair of khakis skimmed his lean, masculine hips as if they were tailor-made. Angel mentally put the cost of his weekend grungies at roughly the cost of her entire fall wardrobe.

''What about your tennis?'' Alex asked mildly from the door of his study as Sandy galloped down the stairs, ramming her arms into a cardigan.

''Oh, I can do that anytime. I mean, Angel *needs* me, don't you, Angel?''

''I can always use more help.''

He frowned, his gaze moving up the staircase to where Angel followed at a slightly more sedate pace. ''If you needed help, why didn't you say so? I can have as many temps as you need sent out if you'll just—''

''I don't need any temps, I already have a man who does my big planting and two part-timers who come in on weekends and after school. But thanks just the same,'' she tacked on grudgingly.

Just like a bloody Hightower. Got a problem? Throw money at it. And because she was being unfair and knew it, Angel made up her mind to do something about his shrubbery before she moved back home. Which would be any day now, even if she had to sleep in a hard hat until Gus declared her premises safe again.

And the shrubs really did need attention. Evidently old Mr. Gilly was no more up to the demands of Hightower's four acres than his wife was of dealing with fourteen rooms. One glance around the grounds and it had been all she could do not to grab her pruning shears and fly into action.

Sandy raced on ahead out the front door, leaving Angel to deal with Alex, who looked mildly ferocious with a scowl and an overnight growth of beard shadowing his jaw. "Are you sure she won't be a nuisance?" he asked.

"I happen to like teenagers." She thought she saw a wintry smile flicker past those cool gray eyes, and wondered if he was thinking of a certain fourteen-year-old pest who had made his life hell a couple of decades ago.

"Well, if you're sure...I'm meeting Carol to go riding later on this morning. Sandy knows the number. Anytime you want me to pick her up, just call."

"Fine. Have a lovely ride." She tried for an airy disdain and came off sounding breathless. Dammit, why did everything have to remind her of a certain pesky lovesick adolescent and the arrogant, elegant, gangling young hunk she had badgered unmercifully for three or four years?

This time it was a genuine smile that kindled in his eyes as he leaned his shoulder against the doorjamb, the paper dangling from his long, square-tipped fingers. "Do you ride, Angel? Why not take a break and go with us? I could probably scare you up some riding gear."

"Thanks, but I really can't spare the time. I do ride, however," she informed him with a glint in her eyes that dared him to question her further.

Actually, she'd only ridden a cow. Once. Aunt Zee had had a friend in the country who kept a milker. Neither Angel nor the cow had cared very much for the experience.

"Perhaps another time, then."

"Perhaps." *And perhaps not.* "Don't worry if we're late. We might stop for barbecue on the way home."

"Look, are you sure you want to do this, Angel? Sandy's a good kid, but I'll be the first to admit she can be a handful when she wants to be. Maybe it would be better if—"

"Oh, for Pete's sake, lighten up, Hightower! I'm not kidnapping your daughter, I'm just taking her across town for a few hours!" Digging her keys out of her shoulder bag, Angel turned and clumped toward the door, the size-five combat boots muffled on the faded splendor of the old Tabriz.

Rattling down University Parkway in the van a few minutes later, with Sandy chattering cheerfully beside her, Angel thought about men and their tendency to go overboard trying to protect what they considered the weaker sex.

Not all men, of course. Some were predators. Some were leaches. Most were chauvinists, but things were changing rapidly in that respect. Not that all the changes were necessarily good.

One of the things that had drawn her to Cal was that he'd encouraged her to be independent. Coming from a family in which women were supposed to stay home and raise kids, cook and keep house—period—Angel had considered him wonderfully enlightened. He had told her right up front that if he married her, he expected her to pull her weight.

More than her weight, as it had turned out. He'd wanted her to pull his, too. But then, Cal had been a user, something she hadn't learned until it was too late.

On the other hand, there was Gus, who hired women as readily as he did men as long as they were qualified. That didn't mean he'd gotten over his habit of rescuing damsels in distress—whether they wanted to be rescued or not, which could be a royal pain.

And then there were men like Alex.

On second thought, there probably weren't any men like Alex. Which was both a shame and a blessing.

"Who else will be there today?" asked Sandy, interrupting Angel's nonproductive train of thought.

"Probably Mac and Bucky, depending on whether or not Bucky has to help his father bale hay. They're both nice. You'll like them."

"Hmm. Maybe. They'll probably think I'm some kind of freak. I guess they're both shorter than I am, huh?"

"Bucky's taller. Mac is only fifteen. He'll probably shoot up in a year or so."

Angel well remembered how terribly insecure she'd been at Sandy's age when it came to meeting new boys. All it took was a few years to get over it, but at fourteen, a year seemed an eternity.

Meanwhile, an understanding parent could help. Hightower needed someone to set him straight on the subject of what was worth hassling over and what wasn't. Men were so dense about some things.

Men were so dense about a *lot* of things.

But then, so were women. About men, in particular. Love could hurt like hell under the best of circumstances. At Sandy's age, with no perspective and no control over burgeoning hormones, it could be worse than PMS and the five-day flu all rolled into one.

"I do like a man with a beard, don't you?" Sandy mused. "Like, I mean, it makes them look so—so manly." She sighed and wriggled her feet in a pair of size ten red Reeboks.

"I'm not sure the ability to grow hair on one's face has all that much to do with being a man, but I know what you mean." Angel thought of the way Alex looked late at night, with a day's growth of stubble. She wondered what it would feel like against the tender skin of her neck, of her breast. "As long as you don't forget that it's character, not hair, that makes a man," she tacked on dutifully.

Sandy snapped her bubble gum. "You sound just like Daddy. Does Gus have a special girlfriend?"

"Not that I know of," Angel admitted, half wishing she could say he did.

"Does he like younger women?"

Fortunately Angel was too busy negotiating the turnoff to answer. She only hoped that Sandy's fascination with beards and scars and older men wouldn't last as long as her own early infatuation had lasted.

Although once Sandy turned her attention back to the Corvette Kid, Alex would *really* have something to worry about!

Mounted on Shadow, his favorite gelding, Alex cantered along the bridle path behind Carol and her small roan mare, fighting the urge to break out in a gallop and cut through the oak grove to the wide pasture beyond.

This urge to break out—to break away—was getting to be a damned nuisance. "Shall we take the shortcut back to the stable?"

"Might as well. I'd forgotten how narrow this trail is. We can't even talk without raising our voices."

Carol never raised her voice. Alex didn't, either—at least, he hadn't until just lately. Nowadays, it didn't take all that much to set him off.

Absently he studied the woman riding before him, one advantage of having chosen the narrower of several bridle trails. She had an excellent seat—hands relaxed, back straight. But then, Carol never did anything that she couldn't accomplish to perfection. It was an art, he supposed. Being good at everything. At ease in every situation.

Unbidden, his thoughts veered to the scene at the breakfast table the first morning Angel had stayed there. She'd come down early, evidently not expecting anyone else to be about. Alex had risen to seat her, his eyes riveted on the pale pink spot on her left cheekbone.

"What happened?" He had pictured her getting up at night in a strange house and blundering into a door or a piece of furniture.

"Zit." She'd scowled at him and reached for the coffeepot.

"I beg your—"

"Calamine, and if you don't mind, I'd just as soon not talk about it."

A *zit?* At *her* age? He'd nearly strangled on his orange juice. And then he'd seen the smile twitching at the corners of her mouth, and he'd really lost it. When Sandy wandered into the room a few minutes later, they'd both been laughing uncontrollably, neither one of them capable of explaining—or even understanding—just what was so funny about a tiny spot dabbed with pale pink lotion.

All he knew was that for a few minutes, he'd felt young again. He'd felt good. It had occurred to him then that he couldn't remember the last time he'd laughed aloud.

After dropping Carol off at her apartment and declining an invitation to stay for lunch, Alex drove by his office, where he buried himself in plans for the upcoming market, and in the paperwork involved with buying out a small, foundering chair company. For once, he'd gone against the advice of his overly conservative directors. He'd had his own reasons, and as those reasons had little to do with Hightower's bottom line, he was having the devil's own time in defending the buy-out.

There were times when he'd like to turn his back on the whole damned furniture business and start over, somewhere new, doing something totally off the wall. Unfortunately, there were some four hundred odd jobs directly depending on his continued good business judgment. Even more once he took over K'ville Chair.

It was later than usual when he got home, his mind on a drink, a swim—although it was getting cool for that—and possibly a nap before dinner. Recently he'd had trouble falling asleep, and even when he did, he'd often wake up about four in the morning, his mind too alert to go back to sleep. Which usually meant he'd be operating at half speed the next day.

He felt restless. Vaguely unsettled. For the life of him, he couldn't put his finger on the reason. The buy-out was right on track. His lawyers were winding up the final agreement now. Granted, he and Sandy were going through a rough patch, but he had no doubt that as long as he could hang on to his patience, they'd come out the other end unscathed.

He was thirty-eight. So maybe it was a mid-life crisis. Or had that only been an eighties thing?

The front door opened onto a square foyer, directly opposite the curving stairway that led to the second floor. The room hadn't changed much since his father's day. Dina hadn't been particularly interested in decorating, and God knows, it was far down on his own list of priorities. He was used to the faded grays and bronzes of the antique rugs, the slightly brighter colors of the stair runner, the Venetian mural done in shades of gray on the side walls, and the hunt table with the vase of whatever flowers happened to be blooming in the back garden—usually shedding leaves and petals on the gleaming cherry surface.

What he wasn't used to was the pair of combat boots parked on the second step, their tops flapped over, with one worn rawhide lace dangling through the banisters. Or the shabby canvas and leather shoulder bag that was draped over the back of one of the side chairs his mother had bought in France on her honeymoon.

Or the sound of giggles and splashes drifting in through the open windows.

He followed the sound to the pool and halted in his tracks, struck by the sight of a lanky beanpole and a small, hippy woman, knees bent in launching position at the far edge of the pool, both laughing too hard to dive.

They'd probably sink like a pair of rocks if they went over now, he thought, half amused, half exasperated. The water was really too cold to swim in. Sandy had been after him to close it in and heat it, and there was no real reason why he shouldn't. He just kept putting off a decision. Lately it was as if his whole life was on hold.

Which was about as crazy a notion as he'd ever had, and he'd had some pretty bizarre ones. Especially over the past few days.

Without conscious thought, he wheeled around, unbuttoning his shirt as he climbed the stairs. Five minutes later, he was down again, wearing trunks, a towel and a pair of sandals.

They were just coming inside. Not even to himself would Alex admit his disappointment. "All done?" he asked with a smile that had to be forced.

"Oh, hi, Daddy! We washed the dirt off in the shower before we went in, so don't worry about the filter. And we got barbecue and stuff for supper, so I told Flora she could go early. She's got an appointment with her chiropractor, but Angel showed her this neat thing you can do with a tennis ball, and about shoes and all, so maybe she won't grunt and groan all the time."

Not a whole lot of this made sense, but Alex was so busy trying to swallow his disappointment, not to mention trying not to goggle at Angel in a faded blue tank suit, that he hardly noticed.

Dina was a beanpole. Carol was a beanpole. His own daughter was a beanpole. Was there something desirable about being skinny? For the life of him, he couldn't figure out why any woman would starve herself and spend half her life sweating in a gym in order to attain beanpole status when small breasts, a tiny waist, flaring hips and well-rounded thighs were so damned lip-licking delectable that one glimpse of them was enough to derail a man's entire train of thought.

"Yeah...what? That is, sure—okay. Whatever you want, sugar."

He did fifteen laps, telling himself he was working the kinks out. When a man spent hours bent over a desk, his neck muscles tended to tighten up.

Right. And when he lay awake half the night imagining the way a certain woman looked underneath a pair of hideous coveralls, a few other muscles tightened up.

Thank God for a swimming pool. First thing tomorrow, he decided, he was going to call in a contractor and see about having the thing heated and enclosed. Now that Angel was back in his life, he had a feeling he was going to be swimming a lot of laps.

Five

It wasn't going to work, Angel told herself. With Gus there to act as a buffer it hadn't been quite so bad, but once he'd left she'd felt like such an outsider. She couldn't do anything right.

For instance, the barbecue. At least once a week, she'd been in the habit of taking home a sliced plate for supper. It was cheap, it was easy, it was delicious. So when Sandy had mentioned the delectable smell of hickory smoke as they'd driven past Charlie's on their way home, she'd pulled in and ordered three plates without giving it a second thought.

It had seemed like a good idea at the time—a token repayment for Alex's hospitality. Only, one did *not* eat barbecue from plastic plates in a formal dining room, under the snooty noses of a flock of ancestral portraits.

So they took the three plates to the breakfast room. Starved from having worked hard all day and then come home and swum the kinks out of her muscles, Angel opened hers up and dug in.

It occurred to her belatedly to wonder if Alex even liked barbecue. She could remember a time when he hadn't been too proud to eat cabbage and corned beef at a kitchen table, but that had been then and this was now.

Another impulse gone awry, she thought resignedly as she salted her fries.

They were discussing the making of fine compost when Alex joined them, his hair still dark from the shower. Evidently he hadn't stayed in the pool very long.

"And then, about every third layer, I add some well-rotted..." Angel glanced up guiltily. "Uh...we didn't wait. I thought you'd be longer."

"No problem."

"I probably should have asked first. About the barbecue, I mean. We drove right past Charlie's Pig Pit and it smelled so good...." The expression pleaded understanding. "I didn't know what you wanted to drink. Sandy said beer. I probably should have left it in the fridge until you finished your swim."

"It's fine. Thank you."

Angel watched his hands as he lifted his heavy stein. He had beautiful hands, long fingered, square tipped, dusted with golden hair. Hands that had figured in more than one of her fantasies. She had more calluses than he did, and his nails were in better shape, but she suspected that there was more strength than was apparent hidden in those hands of his.

The stein had been Sandy's doing. On the rare occasions when Angel drank beer with a meal, she drank it straight from the bottle to save washing a glass. Under Alex's roof, she wouldn't dare do anything so crass. Just one more difference between them. He had probably never in his well-ordered life discussed manure at the dinner table.

But then, she wasn't used to discussing anything over dinner. She usually took hers in the kitchen with the six-o'clock news, her only conversational offering a few rude comments on the political gaffe of the day, plus the occasional prayer to the weather gods.

Thinking of Flora's baked salmon, asparagus and au gratin potatoes, all shoved hastily into the refrigerator, she could have kicked herself for acting so impulsively. Alex had probably been looking forward to it. Not that Flora was such a wonderful cook, but then, anything would taste good served on paper-thin china, with hemstitched linen napkins and sterling flatware that weighed in at five pounds a place setting.

Besides, Angel thought self-righteously, it was her civic duty to support the local economy. Charlie's pig was probably homegrown, and while she didn't know exactly where the salmon had come from, she was pretty sure it hadn't swum up the Eno River.

With that thought tucked firmly in place, she scraped the rounded corners of her foam plate with a plastic spoon and then popped the last sweet hush puppy into her mouth, telling herself she had earned every bite. Potting forty-seven Little Princess spirea, seventeen Purpleleaf sand cherries, and heeling in a row of Spring Snow crab apples was hungry work even without the added exertion of plunging into a chilly swimming pool and trying to keep up with a teenager who swam like an eel.

Tomorrow she was going home, roof or no roof. Alex didn't owe her anything, and now that Gus had left, there was no one to talk her out of it. As soon as he finished his supper—or his dinner, or whatever— she would tell him so before he disappeared to get dressed for the evening. He probably had a date with his blue chip Barbie doll.

Bracing herself to tell him she was moving back home, Angel carried the remains of their dinner out to the kitchen. If she irritated Flora into quitting, Mrs. Gilly would bear the brunt, and the elderly woman, while largely useless, was a dear.

Twenty minutes later, she located Alex in the study. Arms crossed over her chest, she made her announcement from the doorway. "I'll be leaving in the morning. For good, I mean. To go home. Um…thank you for your hospitality."

He studied her silently for a moment, making her feel as if she ought to apologize. "You weren't comfortable here?"

"Of course I'm comfortable here, that's not the point!" she snapped, irritated at being put on the defensive. Damn him, why couldn't he have lost his hair or developed a paunch? Why did he have to look so damned beautiful, with his bony, elegant face and his lean, fit body?

"I take it the carpenters have finished up, then?"

She shrugged. "All but. The electricians will be in first thing tomorrow, but it shouldn't take them long to finish up. It can't be that big a job just to replace a little wiring.''

''Why not stay until Gus gets back to town?''

She could have told him why. That the more she was exposed to him, the harder it was going to be to work him out of her system. That certain childhood afflictions—measles, mumps, love—were far more dangerous when one succumbed as an adult. Any woman with the brains of a thumbtack would cut her risk of exposure.

At odd times during the day, Alex would catch himself thinking about Angel Wydowski instead of the business at hand. About the way she had of laughing. Her laugh hadn't changed much in all these years, yet coming from a woman, the effect was different. Every nerve in his body registered the pitch of that husky little giggle.

When had he memorized the way her eyes crinkled, the way her lips slid over her teeth just before that slow, infectious laughter broke out? Yesterday?

Or twenty years ago?

When had he begun to wonder what her mouth would feel like? What it would taste like? When had he begun to wonder if she would taste the way she smelled, like green, growing things—like flowers and freshly cut grass?

Swearing softly, he jammed his pencil into the electric sharpener. This was crazy! She was nothing to him! The kid sister of an old friend, nothing more. Not even a kid any longer. She had to be somewhere in her early thirties, although she didn't look much older than she had the time she'd gotten hold of a pack of cigarettes, made herself sick and thrown up in the back seat of his new Mustang.

He'd had to clean her up and then talk her out of drowning herself in Jordan Lake.

Angeline Perkins. He wondered what her husband had been like—wondered what had happened to him. Wondered what she'd been like in bed, and then cursed under his breath, buzzed his secretary and told her he'd be out all afternoon.

"Take any messages—tell 'em I'll get back to them. I won't be near a phone for a few hours."

He kept a couple of horses at a boarding stable a few miles out of town. His own gelding and Dina's mare, which Sandy and Carol rode occasionally. He could have kept them on his own property—he had enough acreage—only it hardly seemed worth the trouble.

That was the trouble, he thought with bitter amusement. These days, nothing seemed worth the trouble.

Galloping across the wide dry pasture later in his shirtsleeves and a set of old jodhpurs and boots he kept there for times like these, Alex found his thoughts veering back to the woman he'd come out here to escape.

Angel. Little Devil Wydowski. Was it the novelty that fascinated him? The fact that she was completely unexpected—completely unlike any other woman he knew? Instead of being involved in some respectable white-collar profession, or even dividing her time between volunteer work, the golf course and the club gym, Angel got down and dirty. Quite literally.

He'd come home the second day she'd been there to find her grubbing about in his backyard while old man Gilly held forth on the merits of Mepps spinners versus plastic worms for catching bass. Phil Gilly's idea of heaven included a bass boat, a trolling motor and an endless supply of cheap fortified wines.

Angel. She invariably kicked off her shoes the minute she got into the house. He would find them later on the steps, under the coffee table or tumbled beside a chair, the leather laces sprawled in tangled abandon. She took her diet cola straight from the can, ate French fries with her fingers, and read romance novels without even bothering to hide the covers. And she giggled like a schoolgirl, setting off a lot of crazy impulses that were totally out of character for a dull, middle-aged man with a half-grown daughter.

Although, come to think of it, even Sandy had fallen under her spell, and that was even harder to figure. Sandy didn't make friends easily, especially not with adults. She'd always been shy and a little self-conscious, yet she'd laughed more and sulked less in the few days Angel had been in residence than she had all year.

Feeling the hot September wind in his face as he galloped across the dry pasture, Alex gave up on trying to work the woman out of his system. Like poison ivy—like any other itch—this one would just have to run its course. Meanwhile, he'd do well to remember that scratching an itch could sometimes lead to complications.

Angel. He wondered if she still yelled her head off at baseball games. Gus's life had been football. She'd been a baseball nut. It figured.

Think about something else, man!

The furniture market was coming up in less than a month. He was in the middle of a buy-out, and all he could think of was what it would be like to lay a certain redhead down in the tall grass and rock her bones until they both went up in flames.

The gelding shied as a rabbit darted across the path. Alex managed to stay in the saddle, but a glance at his watch told him he'd already stolen far too much time. He swore with surprising fluency. For all the good it had done him, he might just as well have stayed at the office.

She was gone. He would have known it the minute he walked through the door, even if she hadn't warned him she'd be leaving. The house had that familiar drab, dull, empty feeling he hadn't even noticed before she'd come back into his life. No cola cans on the coffee table. No boots on the stairway. No lumpy canvas shoulder bag slung over the newel post.

No giggles.

For Gus's sake, he should have insisted on driving her home to see if her house was safe for habitation before he let her go. But then, what did he know about such things? Even if he'd put his foot down and insisted she come home with him until Gus got back to give the all clear, she would have just laughed in his face. Small she might be, but the lady had the determination of a diesel locomotive.

Sandy was back to normal. Blaming him for everything that was wrong in her life. "At least you could have begged her to stay," she flung at him over dinner.

"I told her she was welcome here as long as she cared to stay. The choice was hers to make, Sandy."

"Well, it was a rotten choice! And it's all your fault, I don't care what you say, because Angel and me got along just great! She really liked me, too, not like *some* people I could mention, who want to have me locked up in some cruddy old girls' school until I'm a hundred years old!"

"Angel and I."

She glared at him, her lower lip thrust out in a manner reminiscent of her mother. Dina had always been good at sulking. "Angel and you what?"

"I was correcting your grammar," he said tiredly, wishing that for once he'd had the good sense to let it pass.

"Oh, crud, that's all you care about!"

"Don't be crude, Alexandra, and grammar certainly isn't all I care about. I care about you. Only I can't seem to get through to you these days. Is it all my fault, or are you deliberately trying to be difficult?"

Which drew precisely the response he should have anticipated. Sandy flung down her napkin, raked back her chair and raced from the room in tears.

Alex stared unseeingly at his untouched dinner of cold salmon, stringy braised asparagus and cheesy potatoes that tasted as if they'd been reheated. He wondered what would happen if he simply allowed her to curse, butcher the language, dress like a floozy and run wild with the rest of the pack. He wondered if heredity would eventually overcome peer pressure.

He was still wondering a few hours later when Gus showed up.

"Am I glad to see you! Come on in—drop your bag by the stairs. As it happens, I'm in the mood to tie one on for the first time in years."

Gus slung his bag toward the stairs. The Wydowskis were never big on formalities. "If I remember correctly, I nursed you through your first binge. Wanna talk about it before your tongue goes numb?"

"Not to you, old man. Nothing personal." Alex's lips twisted in a bitter smile as he led the way to the study. "Have you had anything to eat? Did you run into any problems? I thought you were going to be gone until the middle of the week."

"Yes, yes and no, in that order. By the way, you sure you don't want to reconsider the binge? You were always a lousy drunk. Better than old Kurt, but neither one of you was much fun on a toot."

"It's cheaper than a shrink. More private, too. How'd the trip go?"

Gus sank down into one of the deep leather chairs that had helped build the reputation of Hightower Fine Furniture, flexed his shoulders and sighed. Alex had always valued privacy. Something to do with being an only child, he figured.

Or maybe not. "The trip went fine. The job is pretty much like one I did up in Kinnakeet Shores last year. I found a place to stay, leased it through December, checked in with a few suppliers who deliver to the Outer Banks and came on back. I had a funny feeling Angel might be getting restless, am I right?"

"Restless and gone. She left this morning. Is it a problem?"

Gus stroked his beard, which was somewhat shaggier than when he'd turned up a little over a week ago.

"Not really. I figured she wouldn't stay away too long. Structurally, I guess the place is sound enough. She probably could have moved home after the second day, but I kind of wanted to get a cleaning crew in first. Not that I wouldn't have had a fight on my hands. One thing the witchlette's never been good at is accepting help. The older she gets, the worse she is in that respect."

Which didn't come as any great surprise. She'd always had a stiff-necked pride that had been amusing when it hadn't irritated the hell out of him. "What about her wiring? Is it safe?"

"Safe enough. Until it's finished, though, it's pretty much of a mess. Walls out, insulation all over the place. The old-fashioned glass wool type, probably. Itches like the very devil. If you're thinking of diving into that bottle, I believe I'll join you."

Alex poured two shots and moved the bottle within reach. "I could go bring her back."

Gus chuckled. "You and whose army?"

"You've got a point."

As the tide in the pinch bottle steadily receded, the two men talked more and more freely. They started out with business, with Alex's going out on a limb to buy a stagnating factory. "Company's privately held, which helps. The family's wanting out from under, but they hate to let down the employees. I happen to be in a position to help out." At Gus's quizzical look, he hurried to say, "Not that it's all one-sided. I'm getting good value for my money."

"Sure you are. A sinking wreck of a plant that probably needs a complete retooling and overhaul to come up to minimum standards. It's a rescue mission, man—admit it.''

"Don't confuse me with Kurt. Is he still flying rescue missions for the Coast Guard?"

"As far as I know. But Alex, face it. This is a bailout, plain and simple. I remember a time when you were all set to study medicine and save the world. Then your old man blackmailed you into taking over the family business, and now you're trying to make it up by playing the corporate Albert Schweitzer, right?"

"Crap.'' So what if he'd nurtured a dream for a little while? All kids did. As an only son, he'd never been allowed to forget his responsibility. Children—particularly only children—were the repository of their parents' dreams. "Yeah? What about you? I understand you consistently overorder materials and then pass on the extras to some charity home-building outfit."

Gus shrugged. "So sue me."

"Dues-paying time, right? So no more cracks about my little business venture. I get enough flak from my board of directors."

"That I can believe. What's the bottom line?"

"It's a wash. The initial capital outlay probably won't affect our stock. We'll have to do some retooling, sure, but not as much as you might think. It's a labor-intensive operation. In the long run, we'll be breaking into a new market."

"Meanwhile, a one-mule town will survive and a lot of people who're too old to find other work will go on bringing in a paycheck for a few more years. Not to mention the added comfort of the generous Hightower benefits package. Am I right, Dr. Schweitzer?"

Alex shrugged. "Like I said—it's a wash."

They were silent for several moments, both men thinking of roads not taken. After a while, Gus said, "Sometimes I wonder if I'm not spreading myself too thin, taking contracts at both ends of the state instead of settling down in one area. I'm on the road so damned much, I've even considered buying a plane and learning to fly. Maybe Kurt could be talked into coming back home and taking the job."

Inevitably the talk moved into more personal channels. Alex voiced a few of his doubts about getting further involved with Carol. "She reminds me a lot of Dina, and God knows, I fell like a ton of bricks for her. Dina, I mean—not Carol."

"Who didn't?" Gus commented wryly, which was as close as he had ever come to admitting that the reason he'd left town right after Alex and Dina had married was because he'd been so damned blind, stupid in love with Alex's bride.

Kurt had, too. Not that any of the three of them had ever discussed it.

As for Gus, he'd known right from the first that he didn't have a snowball's chance in hell, even if Dina hadn't already set her sights on Alex. He wasn't handsome like Kurt, or wealthy like Alex. Looks, wealth and pedigree were important to women like Dina Hathaway-Addams Hightower Whatever. The Wydowskis were strictly blue-collar, and had never pretended to be anything else.

All the same, for a while there, he'd almost hated Alex for being who and what he was—for being the man Dina had chosen. Gus had fallen in love twice in his life, both times with women who were not only ineligible, but way the hell out of his league. Which proved, he supposed with a bleak sort of amusement, that he had excellent taste.

"No law says a man has to marry," Gus mused after a while.

"Sandy needs a mother. She's dropped a few heavy hints in the last few days."

"Somehow, I can't see your friend Carol in the role."

"Neither can Sandy. Unfortunately."

They drank silently for a few minutes, each lost in private thoughts. And then Alex said, "I guess it's no secret that Dina and I didn't always get along so well."

With a short bark of laughter, Gus said, "Seeing's how she's currently the high muckety-muck of whatchamacallit, I figured something of the sort. It happens, I guess." At least Alex had had a shot at it. If it had been him, he'd never in a million years have let her go. Which just went to show that a guy could be smart in some ways and dumb as wet plaster in others.

"It was mostly my fault. The split, I mean. D'you know something? We never talked. I'm a pretty boring guy—Dina said so. Said it more'n once. Funny thing, though—we found plenty to talk about before we were married."

"Yeah," Gus said dryly. "If I remember correctly, you were always telling her how beautiful her eyes were, and how great she looked in whatever she happened to be wearing, and what a lucky son of a bitch you were to have her."

It was Alex's turn to laugh. "I was never that bad."

"Believe me, you were worse. I never heard an intelligent sentence out of you the whole time you two were dating. Not that I blamed you. Guess we all sorta fell for Lady Dina—she was a classy broad.''

Alex waved his glass, which was fortunately too near empty to spill over. ''Hey, watch what you call my ex-wife, Wydowski!''

Sighing heavily, Gus stared down at the knees of his rumpled khakis. ''Least you've got Sandy. Man needs kids. Family. Something to work for.''

''Gus, you wanna know something real sad? I can't talk to Sandy, either. God knows I love her, but I can't seem to get in touch with her head anymore. We used to be close—she used to do her homework while I read the paper—we used to talk about everything. Funny thing, though—she never talked much about Dina.''

Gus nodded sagely. ''Figures. Kid's mother walks out, leaves her flat—must hurt like hell. Angel got that way a few months after she married that bastard, Perkins. Clammed right up. Smiled too much, and never said anything. What was that old blues number? 'She nev-er said a mum-ba-lin' word,''' he sang tunelessly.

Alex lifted the bottle, changed his mind and set it down again. ''What was he like?''

''Who?''

''Perkins.''

''Oh, him. A real jerk. Good-looking, I guess. Women always seem to go for the type. Angel was on the rebound, else she'd have seen through him. Didn't even know the bastard but a few months before she married him.''

Alex didn't want to hear it. It was none of his business, but Gus's tongue had loosened up, and as a dutiful host, he told himself solemnly, it was his duty to listen.

"First guy who hurt her real bad—you probably know the slimeball, so I won't mention any names. He started coming on to her right after you and Dina got married. Hell, she was still just a kid. I'd already left town, else I'd have done something about it. You know Angel—straight as a narrow—um, an arrow. Never even occurred to her that the bastard was just playing games."

"I don't think I want to hear this," Alex said.

"Yeah, well maybe I need to talk about it, so just shut up and listen, will you? You owe me for all that slushy crap you used to spout about Dina until Kurt threatened to cram a pair of sweat socks down your throat." Gus poured himself another drink, his movements only slightly unsteady. Setting it aside, he said, "Angel thought the bastard wanted to marry her. Like I said, he was smooooth. By the time he dumped her, she was in pretty bad shape. Time I came through town about a week later, she looked like hell warmed over. Didn't say much, but I could tell something was baaad wrong. I finally found out what had happened from one of her friends. I was all set to shove his ass to the altar with the barrel of a shotgun."

Alex scowled, his pink-rimmed eyes not quite focused. "Who is he? I'll murder the bastard."

"Not worth it. B'lieve me, after checking him out, I decided she'd got off pretty easy. He's a user. You know the type. An' you know Angel, my frien'." His words were beginning to slur around the edges by now. "Knock her down, she jus' comes back fightin'. Ol' Ange, she decides to show him she don't give a sweet damn in hell by marrying Perkins, only Perkins is cut from the same bolt of cloth. I know for a fact he ran around on her. I don't know how much she knew, but she must've 'spected something when he wrapped his truck around a tree on his way home from a party with some bimbo.''

Alex muttered a word he hadn't used in a dozen years.

"Word around the patrol station was that Perkins was half out of his pants when it happened. I was able to keep that much off the record, at least, thanks to a couple of friends from our old Wolfpack days."

Alex, soberer than he had any right to be under the circumstances, swore softly.

"All in all, I guess she took it pretty well. She's tough, my little sister. Trouble is, she's not quite as tough as she tries to make out." Gus stirred and rose stiffly from the leather and feather-cushioned *bergère*. "Reckon I'd better go call while I can still dial a phone, see if she's managed to burn the place down again."

Six

There was nothing at all of Alex in his daughter as far as Angel could see, except for her coloring. If newspaper pictures and that glitzy spread in *Uptown* could be believed, the poor child was Dina through and through, Angel thought dismally.

So why do I like her?

"Junipers come in all sizes and shapes. These squishy ones over here are called blue rug juniper. They're great for banks and ground covers. Those tall ones over there are columnar junipers. They've got a Latin name, too, but it's a mouthful."

Sandy had hitched a ride out with one of her teachers, and after assuring Angel that she had her father's permission, she'd made a beeline for the field where the boys were heeling in new arrivals. Once they'd gone home, she'd wandered over to the shed and started moaning again about the fact that she was too tall, too skinny and her feet were too big.

"You have to remember, Sandy, it takes all sizes and shapes to make a beautiful garden. Too much of any one thing would be boring."

"You're like, trying to make me feel better, right?" Crouching over the tray of succulents Angel had been labeling, Sandy nibbled a thumbnail, grimaced at the taste and wiped her hands on the seat of her jeans.

"Hey, gardening's my business. I never joke about business."

"Mrs. Gilly says we have to take what the good Lord gives us and be grateful it isn't worse, but I mean, why couldn't He've given me a bosom while He was at it?"

"He's probably saving it for your sixteenth birthday present."

"Oh, sure, when I'll be too old to care. I'm the only girl in my class at school who has to stuff her training bra, and—oh, darn, here comes Daddy! Why did he have to come after me?" Sandy's gaze strayed toward the house, where Gus was talking to the electrical inspector. "I thought you and Gus were going to take me home."

Gus had arrived in town the night before, but only shown up at Angel's place a few hours ago, obviously hung over. She knew he'd spent the night at Alex's but hadn't asked any questions.

Rising, Angel dusted off her knees, scattering bits of pine bark mulch, as Alex sauntered over, looking tired and impatient and altogether too attractive in a lightweight gray suit with a rumpled tie tugged loose from his collar and a shadow of beard darkening his stubborn jaw.

Come to think of it, he looked a bit hung over, too.

He greeted his daughter, but his gaze homed directly on Angel. "I see you made it through the night with no major disasters."

Darn it, it wasn't fair. Even his voice was a stealth weapon. Her chin ratcheted up another notch. "You sound surprised." She braced herself as all the old familiar symptoms set in—the shuddery feeling in her chest, the tingling between her thighs and the sudden tightness of her nipples. So far, he hadn't so much as smiled at her. Heaven help her if he ever actually laid a hand on her!

He used to laugh, flashing those big, white teeth. Now he seldom even smiled. He had changed so much over the years while she'd watched from a distance, and yet, the essential Alex had to be in there somewhere under all those well-bred suits, those white-on-white monogrammed shirts and polished cordovans. Even back in his high school and early college days, when he'd been a rough and rugged defensive lineback, there'd been something special about him. Something strong, modest, honorable, and noble—all the old knight-in-shining-armor virtues that seemed to have disappeared about the same time Camelot had been bulldozed and turned into a shopping mall.

Angel told herself that the knight was still hiding in there somewhere. His sword might be a little duller and his armor considerably more battered, but then, that was the dragon business for you.

She went on labeling succulents. "You're expected for dinner tonight," he reminded her. "Did Gus tell you?"

Angel nodded silently. She had no intention of subjecting herself to any further temptation. Gus could go to dinner. At the last minute, she fully intended to have a headache.

Gus sauntered up, looking only a little bit paler than usual. "Hey, you didn't have to battle traffic, man. We could've taken Sandy home with us."

"I was in the neighborhood."

Gus lifted one brow. Angel concentrated on the clump of composted cow manure on the toe of her left boot. Sandy heaved an exaggerated sigh and slogged off to the office, where she'd left her schoolbooks.

"He's got a handful in that young lady," Gus mused a few minutes later as brother and sister stood side by side outside the greenhouse, watching them drive off in Alex's XJ6.

"Fourteen's a rough age. She'll come through just fine, though. Sandy's a very special young lady. By the way, I'm not going with you tonight."

Pursing his lips in a silent whistle, Gus said, "I was afraid of that."

"It's no big deal. I feel a headache coming on, that's all."

"Too bad. I used up all your aspirin. And anyhow, unless I miss my guess, this particular headache has been coming on for about twenty years, right?"

She glared at him. "Did my electrical pass muster?"

"Good as new. Better. I had 'em put in a heavier service. This old place was built in the forties when all

SILHOUETTE®

AN IMPORTANT MESSAGE FROM THE EDITORS OF SILHOUETTE®

Dear Reader,

Because you've chosen to read one of our fine romance novels, we'd like to say "thank you"! And, as a **special** way to thank you, we've selected <u>four more</u> of the <u>books</u> you love so well, **and** a Porcelain Trinket Box to send you absolutely *FREE!*

Please enjoy them with our compliments...

Luna Macro

Senior Editor,
Silhouette Desire

P.S. And because we value our customers, we've attached something extra inside ...

EDITOR'S
FREE
GIFT
SEAL
THANK YOU

PEEL OFF SEAL AND
PLACE INSIDE

HOW TO VALIDATE YOUR
EDITOR'S FREE GIFT "THANK YOU"

1. Peel off gift seal from front cover. Place it in space provided at right. This automatically entitles you to receive four free books and a beautiful Porcelain Trinket Box.

2. Send back this card and you'll get brand-new Silhouette Desire® novels. These books have a cover price of $3.75 each, but they are yours to keep absolutely free.

3. There's no catch. You're under no obligation to buy anything. We charge nothing—ZERO—for your first shipment. And you don't have to make any minimum number of purchases—not even one!

4. The fact is thousands of readers enjoy receiving books by mail from the Silhouette Reader Service™ months before they're available in stores. They like the convenience of home delivery and they love our discount prices!

5. We hope that after receiving your free books you'll want to remain a subscriber. But the choice is yours—to continue or cancel, anytime at all! So why not take us up on our invitation, with no risk of any kind. You'll be glad you did!

6. Don't forget to detach your FREE BOOKMARK. And remember…just for validating your Editor's Free Gift Offer, we'll send you FIVE MORE gifts, *ABSOLUTELY FREE!*

YOURS FREE!

*This beautiful porcelain box is topped with a lovely bouquet of porcelain flowers, perfect for holding rings, pins or other precious trinkets — and is yours **absolutely free** when you accept our no risk offer!*

you needed was a radio, a fan, a few lights and an ice-box. At least now you can operate a decent-size hot water heater."

"Fine. And since you're going out tonight, you might as well have the first shower. Once I finish up here, I intend to soak my bones until they stop aching."

"I thought it was your head that was aching."

"Are you telling me to go soak my head?"

He grinned, looking considerably younger than his thirty-nine years in spite of the touch of gray in his dark hair. "Change your mind and come with me tonight, Angel. You're all grown-up now. Alex can't hurt you."

He watched the light go out of her eyes and cursed his own careless words. He knew how it felt. Fortunately, his own pain had lessened over the years until it was little more than scar tissue now. The trouble with Angel was that she kept on jumping back into the ring and getting her wounds reopened, first by that tennis-playing bastard who'd looked enough like Alex to be a cousin but wasn't. Gus had checked him out thoroughly. And then by Perkins, who at least had had the decency to marry her.

Not that that had turned out to be any great blessing. He didn't know if there'd been any others—he rather thought not, because he suspected that through it all, his little sister had been carrying a pretty big torch for Alex.

Evidently she still was.

Angel hadn't come. Alex freely admitted to being disappointed. It was the depth of his disappointment

that worried him. To make up for it, he went all out to
appear convivial. He made a point of including Sandy
in the table talk, and was rewarded by her occasional
ingenuous comments on current affairs. Gus beamed
like a proud uncle and Alex thought, she's growing up.
In spits and spurts, with frequent lapses, his little girl
was definitely growing up.

Gus was telling them about a recent horseback riding experience that had ended up in his being tossed
down a ravine and being confronted by an old woman
with a double-barrel shotgun who took him for a federal agent out to burn her marijuana patch.

"Oh, do you like horses?" Sandy asked, brighten-
ing. "Daddy has this mare named Tansy that used to
belong to Mama. I ride her sometimes. We could go
riding. I could ride Tansy and you could borrow
Shadow, couldn't he, Daddy? How about Saturday?"

Alex was caught between amusement and irritation. "Maybe Gus has other plans for the weekend,
princess," he suggested mildly.

"Matter of fact, it sounds like fun. Why don't we
make up a party—you two and Angel and me. If
someone doesn't pry Angel away from that mud hole
of hers, she'll work herself to the bone. Trouble is, she
never learned how to play."

Sandy obviously hadn't planned on a foursome, not
with her father making up the numbers. "But doesn't
she have to be there on Saturdays?"

"The boys can cover for her while she takes off a
few hours."

"Oh. Okay, then Daddy can rent a couple more
horses and we can take the back trail—it's wider, and

I can show you where Tansy flushed a covey of bob-
whites and almost threw me last fall."

Alex wondered if Gus knew what he was letting
himself in for. Sandy could talk the hind end off a
jackrabbit when she was wound up. And she was
nearly always wound up when Gus was around. "I'll
call in the morning and make arrangements," he said.
"Gus, I'll leave it to you to arrange things with Angel."

Saturday dawned crisp and clear, the sky a deep
October blue even though September wasn't quite
over. Alex had always liked autumn. For reasons he'd
never bothered to explore, it had always seemed more
of a beginning than an ending. But this time the feeling of excited expectancy faded quickly when Angel
declined to join them.

"Sure you won't change your mind? We'll just be
out a couple of hours." Dammit, he refused to beg!

"Sorry—I've got these Lombardy poplars that need
to be heeled in, and the forecast is for rain on Monday."

Alex hung up the phone, irritated. More than irritated. He was mad as hell! Without stopping to think,
he dialed Carol's number and put the proposition to
her.

"Riding? Oh, well...I was on my way out the door,
but I can shop later. Give me half an hour to change,"
she said, and he wished he'd let well enough alone.
He'd had this stupid notion in the back of his mind
about proving something to himself, only it wasn't
working. Carol was no substitute for Angel. Not in a
million years.

"Meet us at the stables, then—say, forty-five minutes?"

"Us?" Carol was saying when he hung up.

They could have made it a threesome. He'd rather have made it a twosome. Himself and Angel. Gus was right, she worked too hard. She couldn't be all that hung up on horticulture—the Angel he remembered from his high school days wouldn't have known the difference between a rose and a rutabaga. Or cared.

They met at the stables. Carol, as usual, looked like a cover model for *Equestrienne* magazine. Sandy wore jeans and a sweatshirt. She wore a hard hat, but only under protest. It was another of those "Oh, *Daa*-ddy!" things.

"Why don't we start out on the back trail?" Carol suggested. "Come on, Gus, I'll show you the way." Her sidelong glance toward Alex was teasing. "You two don't mind bringing up the rear, do you?"

The tip of Sandy's nose was turning suspiciously red, a sure sigh that she was either about to cry, or to let fly with a full-fledged temper tantrum. Alex set his mind to distracting her.

"Whatever happened to your friend with the Corvette?"

God, he'd had to go and remind her? His batteries obviously needed recharging.

"Arvid? He's been grounded for a month," she said dismissively. "He's pretty dumb, anyhow. Not like *some* boys I know who get jobs on weekends."

Alex felt as if things might be starting to look up.

"Look at her! You know what I wish? I wish Tansy would ride her under a branch and knock that silly smirk off her face!"

Alex's shoulders slumped. Shadow, sensing his distraction, began to act up but was quickly brought under control. "If you're not enjoying yourself, Alexandra, I can drive you home right now."

"I just don't see why Angel couldn't have come, that's all!"

"She was invited. She had other things to do. Ease up, you're making your mount nervous."

"Yes, well, *she's* making me nauseous!" Alex didn't make the mistake of thinking she was referring to the rented mare. Maybe he ought to take the time to sort out a few things right then and there. He could understand Sandy's disappointment. He could even understand her feelings toward Carol, but that didn't excuse bad manners.

Suddenly the bright autumn sky seemed slightly tarnished. Monday's promised rain in the offing, he told himself. It had nothing at all to do with the pair chattering cheerfully up ahead. And certainly nothing to do with the sullen adolescent plodding along beside him.

They came to a wide place, where lightning had taken out a big red oak a few months earlier, and before he could call her back, Sandy was off and running. With barely enough room to pass, she galloped past Gus's startled gelding and called over her shoulder, "Race you to the fence, Gus!"

The little fool. Oh, God, the little brat! Alex took off after her, with Gus only half a length behind, while Carol tried to control her mare.

"Dammit, girl—" was all he had time to cry before she reached the split rail fence, which was an easy jump under normal conditions.

Conditions were anything but normal, however. The mare was skittish, and Sandy wasn't ready. Her pacing was off. By the time she realized she wasn't going to make it, it was already too late. She went sailing over the mare's head just as Alex hurled himself off Shadow's back and ran the last few yards to the crumpled figure in jeans and a hot pink sweatshirt.

Gus was right on his heels. He knelt down on the other side of the limp form lying in a bed of what looked suspiciously like poison ivy. "Easy there, baby—no, don't try to get up, just concentrate on breathing—attagirl."

"Easy, princess, Daddy's here. I've got you now, don't cry."

Carol stopped a few yards away, not dismounting. "Oh, for God's sake, she's not hurt, any fool can see that."

Ignoring her, Gus continued to trace her limbs. "Okay here—hmm, nothing here, but her left leg—"

"Yeah, I know. Easy now, sweetheart, don't try to move, Daddy's got you."

The two men briskly discussed the urgency of splitting her boot and of calling 911. Alex cursed his choice of trails—this was the most inaccessible of them all—while Carol stalked back and forth, muttering about silly children showing off. Quickly a plan of action was agreed on. The boot remained intact to serve as bracing, particularly as neither man had a knife that was sharp enough to insure cutting through leather without doing further injury to the patient. Alex mounted Shadow and Gus lifted a white-faced Sandy carefully up into his arms, taking particular care not to jar her leg. Then Gus raced off ahead to the stable to call an ambulance.

Carol was largely ignored.

It was nearly six when Angel locked up the office, adjusted the lights in the greenhouse and headed for the bathtub and whatever she could find in the refrigerator. Which, considering the fact that she hadn't had time to shop for groceries since her power had been restored, wouldn't be much.

Gus still wasn't back. Off and on during the day, she told herself that she might as well have gone with him for all the advantage she'd gained by staying. She'd sold two Bradford pears and one tray of chrysanthemums. But at least she'd had better sense than to set herself up for another fall. Besides which, the new stock was taken care of.

They must be having a wonderful time, she thought ruefully. Riding, having lunch together—probably swimming in the afternoon and lying around the pool, lazily soaking up the unseasonably warm sunshine and talking over old times.

She could have been a part of it all, if it weren't for her pigheaded refusal to let go of an old dream. She and Hightower had known each other forever, for heaven's sake! What was more natural than for old friends, meeting again after so long, to spend time together catching up on old times?

Hogwash.

She wanted to spend time with him all right. Preferably in a king-size bed. Or maybe a swimming pool, under a half-moon, with a privacy fence a mile high and a foot thick.

Passing the refrigerator, she swigged down half a can of flat diet cola, filled the basket and pot and plugged in the coffee maker, then headed for the bathroom, which had been tacked on to the house after it had been built by closing off a portion of the back porch. Hardly a convenient arrangement, but it served well enough.

Half an hour later, she let herself out the bathroom door, hugging a voluminous terry-cloth robe around her. Once the sun set, the air had turned distinctly chilly. It smelled of cookouts, burning leaves and flowering *Elaeagnus,* a heady combination. She had lingered in the open stretch of porch between the bathroom and kitchen doors to watch the moon lift over the top of the greenhouse. She was still there when Alex drove into the yard, pulling right up to the edge of the back steps.

Suddenly acutely aware of her own nakedness under Cal's old bathrobe, she shivered. "Hi. Where's Gus?" she called out softly, instinctively seeking to preserve the spell of moonlight, spicy autumn air and Alex. If this was a dream and she was still sleeping, she'd just as soon not wake herself up.

"Baby-sitting." Propping one foot on the bottom step, Alex explained the circumstances. "I hate like the devil to ask it of you, Angel, but Mrs. Gilly can't take the stairs, and the agency can't send anyone out until Monday, so I thought—that is, it's only tonight and tomorrow—and maybe tomorrow night. I washed her the best I could in case she landed in poison ivy, but she needs a woman to finish the job."

Angel didn't want to go for the simple reason that she wanted it too much. "I don't know—I'm not much good in a sickroom."

"She's not sick, she's just sore. It's a bad sprain, not a break. The trouble is, she can't get out of bed, and you know how kids are at that age. She's already bored with TV, and I'm afraid if you can't help out, Carol's going to insist on staying. She's already dropped a few hints."

"So?"

Alex shifted position. In the dim light spilling through the kitchen window, he looked tired and harried. There were circles under his eyes and the shadow of a beard on his stubborn jaw. It was all Angel could do not to gather him in her arms and hug the stuffing out of him.

"Maybe that would be the best solution," she suggested gently.

The best for her, at least. She wasn't cut out to play the martyr.

"Sorry. I didn't mean to put you on the spot."

"But you don't think Carol's presence will help very much, right?" She was deliberately jumping into a quicksand bog.

"I take it Sandy's said something to you."

"About Carol? She mentioned that they don't always see eye-to-eye."

"Yeah—well, that's an understatement."

How do you feel about her? How do you feel about me? Am I anything more than a handy household appliance? Plug me in, switch me on, and I look after whatever needs looking after until you switch me off and stash me back in the utility room.

He was still wearing riding gear. Angel suspected he'd had a rugged few hours of it. "Look, come on in and have a cup of coffee while I get dressed. I made fresh, and—oh, phoo, I can't even offer you a bagel. I haven't had time to shop yet."

Seven

When had she managed to take over his life? Alex wondered, half amused, half irritated. Not to mention half aroused. It seemed to be a permanent state ever since Angel Wydowski had backed into his life again.

Dammit, she had scarcely been under his roof for twenty-four hours this time, and already she was bossing his staff, planning shopping trips with his daughter and talking to Phil Gilly about reseeding the lawn and converting a section down from the pool to a vegetable garden.

He was quietly going out of his mind, wanting her, and she was thinking about vegetable gardens!

Gus had insisted on staying out at her place overnight to keep an eye on it. He'd confided in Alex that before he left town again, he had arranged for a cleaning crew to come in and give the place a thorough going-over.

Not that it would help all that much. The place was a dump. After seeing that pathetic excuse for a bathroom tacked on to her back porch, Alex was ready to move her out of there permanently.

More than that—he wasn't ready to think about.

The sound of laughter drifted downstairs to the study, where he had adjourned after breakfast to go over the final plans for the fall market display next month. It had never occurred to him that the sound of Sandy's laughter was so rare until Angel had brought laughter back to his home.

When had things grown so grim around here? Was it because he was tied up so much with business? Or was he tied up so much with business because things were so grim at home?

On Sunday afternoon, Carol came over to bring the invalid a bouquet of balloons and a Disney video. Alex remembered taking her to see the movie when she was about seven. She had loved it then. She was less than enchanted now, although to her credit, she didn't say so.

"Thank you. I've always loved this one."

"Yes, well, I thought you might be bored."

"Oh, I'm not really bored. I mean, my ankle throbs, but Angel says that's only a sign that it's getting better."

"Angel?"

"Angel Perkins. You remember—you met her here the other night?"

"She's been to see you?"

"She's staying here. Didn't Daddy tell you?"

Daddy had obviously not told her. "Well. I suppose you'll be able to hobble back to school tomorrow, so there's no real need for a baby-sitter."

Alex strolled in in time to see his daughter widen her eyes in exactly the same way Dina used to. The way Carol sometimes did for effect. He had caught Dina practicing in front of a mirror once early in their marriage, and she'd confessed it was a trick she'd learned from a sorority sister.

But where the hell had Sandy picked it up?

"Oh, Angel's not a baby-sitter," she said airily. "She's my friend. Daddy's known her forever, you know. She's doing all sorts of great stuff around here. Like, you know how Flora always cooks all this gunky, greasy stuff for breakfast? She's going to take care of that, and you know those trees that shed all over the pool? She's outside right now with Mr. Gilly, whacking off what needs whacking."

Alex didn't know whether to laugh or to ground the brat for the next ten years. She was doing it deliberately. Carol had always been territorial. Lately she'd been getting intense about it. Come to think of it, she was the one who had recommended Flora, who was an indifferent cook, but who was reliable and didn't mind Mrs. Gilly's officiousness.

"Sandy, don't you think it's time you had a nap?" he suggested quietly from the doorway.

"Da-addy, I've been in bed forever! I don't need a nap, what I need is for you or Gus to take me out by the pool where I can watch Angel and Mr. Gilly. How am I ever going to learn anything about tree stuff stuck up here all day?"

"Gus is out at the nursery supervising a cleaning crew, and it's too cool for you to sit outside. It's clouded up and turned windy. Carol? How about a drink before you leave?"

"Oh, am I leaving? I thought I might invite myself to dinner. I'm sure Flora can deal with one extra guest on short notice."

He should have known it wasn't going to be so easy.

Gus got back just before dinner to report on the status of Perkins Landscaping & Nursery. Evidently he'd pitched in with the crew and done a bit of cleaning himself, because he was looking distinctly grimy in an ancient pair of jeans and a filthy sweatshirt, the sleeves shoved up on his muscular arms.

Carol leaned back in her chair, adjusted her skirt to reveal several more inches of slender nylon-clad leg and did the eye thing for him.

Women, thought Alex. They had to be born that way.

Although, come to think of it, he'd never caught Angel in any such obvious tricks. If she was attracted to a man, she would damn well do something about it. Even as a kid, back when she'd had this childish crush on him, she had wriggled her way between him and whatever girl he'd been dating at the time every chance she got, beaming up at him as proudly as if she'd pulled off a major coup.

"Isn't that right, Alex?"

"Beg pardon?"

"Gus was saying Angel's little place is in first-class condition now, and I told him she was probably dying to get home."

"Oh. Yeah. Maybe." *Brilliant, Hightower. No wonder you've been kicked upstairs in your own company.*

Carol stayed for dinner. Gus showered, changed into fresh khakis and a black knit shirt, and set out to entertain her, which was a good thing, because Alex couldn't seem to keep his mind on any conversation for more than three minutes in succession.

Angel was having a tray upstairs with Sandy. Every now and then he could hear a shout of laughter all the way downstairs.

"Heavens, what on earth is going on up there? Shouldn't Sandy be resting? You'd think some people would have sense enough not to—oh, dear." She swept Gus a look of apology.

Alex bit back a retort and rose, suggesting they adjourn to the study, which had the advantage of not being located directly below Sandy's bedroom.

It was just after ten when Gus offered to follow Carol home to be sure she arrived safely. Carol hesitated, and Alex could practically follow her thought processes.

Physically, she'd be thinking, Gus was an attractive man, but he was only a carpenter, after all—not even a developer. On the other hand, a bit of competition might make Alex sit up and take notice. But what if she allowed him to follow her home and he asked to come in for a drink? What if he wanted something more than a drink? Would it be worth the bother?

Not really. Not for Carol. Alex knew her too well, had known her ever since kindergarten, through both their marriages and divorces. If there was one thing he was certain of, it was that Carol had no more real interest in the physical side of any man-woman relationship than Dina had. She might covet the position of wife to a successful and presentable man for the simple reason that socially a single woman was at a disadvantage, but conjugal duties fell pretty far down on her list of priorities.

He almost grinned when she yawned and said, "Thanks, dear, but no thanks. I'll call as soon as I get home."

Both men saw her to her car. "Nice-looking woman," Gus observed as they watched her drive off.

"Mmm-hmm."

"She's got the hots for you."

"The lukewarms for me. The hots for my position, whatever the hell that is." Alex shrugged, and they turned to go back inside.

The door hadn't quite closed behind them when a small figure wearing a pair of red flannel pajamas that clashed horribly with her hair, came hurtling down the banister. A split second before her backside collided with the newel post, she rolled off, landing on her bare feet.

Turning, Angel caught sight of her audience. "Oh, no," she groaned. "I heard the door—I thought you'd gone to take Carol home." A study in shades of red, pink and orange, she shot Alex a mortified look.

"You mean you wouldn't have minded if Gus had caught you?"

"Oh, well...he's seen me before. It, um...it's a great way to polish the banister." She looked guilty as sin and cute as a baby duck. In the yawning silence, she blurted, "But I won't do it again if you don't want me to. I never—I mean, almost never—and really, I only did it because I've never had access to a curved one before. Most of them are too short and too steep, and then there are those jig-a-jag ones with posts and corners every few feet. You can't get up any momentum at all on those, and besides, they're downright dangerous."

She looked from one to the other. "Gus? Alex? *Say* something!"

"Is she always like this?" Not a flicker of expression marred Alex's bony features, although inside he was grinning from ear to ear.

"Yep. You don't want to see her at the fair. She'll wear you plum to a frazzle. I've seen her fight little kids for the last place on one of those whiz-a-ma-gizmos."

"That's a lie!" Angel marched forward to confront the pair of them, hands on her hips.

Alex couldn't recall when he'd enjoyed anything quite so much. Or when anyone had looked so completely out of place in the somber foyer with its faded Oriental rug, its gray Venetian mural and its stiff-backed side chairs with their drab tapestry seats.

She made it come alive. She made *him* come alive. And while he didn't wish his daughter a prolonged recovery, he wished to hell he could think of some excuse to keep this small, amazing woman from walking out of his life again.

At least until he could figure out why he wanted her in it.

"Did you need something from downstairs, or was this just a dry run?" Three shades of red, he mused, still struggling to keep from laughing. Although to be precise, her face was more of a deep pink.

"Sandy's still hungry. The chicken was tough and the cake was, um, pretty dry."

It had been stale. Alex had eaten it anyway. He'd never been particularly interested in food, as long as it appeared at regular intervals without his having to go to too much trouble. "Be my guest," he said, with a gracious gesture toward the back of the house.

A motion at the head of the stairs caught his eye. "What the devil—? Dammit, Alexandra, you're not supposed to stand on that ankle!"

"But, Daddy, I'm not standing on my ankle, I'm standing on my foot."

"Don't be impertinent!"

"Sorry. You guys were like, talking so much, I thought I'd join the party."

Scowling, Alex headed for the stairs. Gus brushed past him. "You handled Carol. This one's mine." Sweeping her up in his arms, he turned and carried her down the stairs. "Okay, brat, you're invited, but no food fights, y'hear? And no dancing on the kitchen table."

Suddenly it really was a party. Alex was reminded of his high school days, and the impromptu gatherings at the Wydowski household. He remembered feeling vaguely guilty because he'd never encouraged his friends to gather at his home. The Wydowskis had been a noisy, cheerful, gregarious bunch, including Gus's Aunt Zee, who did things with cards and Ouija boards, and was always guessing someone's sun sign— usually correctly.

His own home, while it had been pleasant enough, with his mother, a gracious, lovely lady setting the tone, had always been quiet, orderly...

And dull.

They found ice cream in the freezer, which went a long way toward resurrecting the last of the stale pound cake. Angel chopped what was left of the cold baked chicken and added a few more ingredients, and they heaped the resulting curried chicken salad on split toasted rolls and washed it down with Gus's high-test coffee.

"You know you're never going to get to sleep again, don't you, young'un?" Gus teased. "I can see you perched in your rocking chair fifty years from now, your hair all stringy and gray, your beady eyes still staring like a pfoo bird, your—"

"What's a phoo bird?" asked Sandy as she absently scratched the single spot of poison ivy that had erupted the day after her fall.

"Gus, don't you dare!" Angel exclaimed.

Alex grinned. And then he chuckled. "Good Lord, is that old joke still around? I haven't heard that one in twenty years."

"Tell me, tell me, tell me!" Sandy squealed.

"I'm afraid it's not for mixed company, princess."

"*Da*-addy! I'm practically grown-up! I bet I know jokes that would make you blush!"

"I don't doubt it for a minute, but I'd just as soon not hear them."

"*An*-gel! Make him tell me! It's not fair!"

Angel, busy scraping the last smidge of ice cream from the bottom of her dish, shrugged her shoulders. "Sorry, hon. I don't make the rules, I only follow 'em. Rules say you have to be sixteen before you can share scatological jokes with a parent. It's one of those dumb authority things."

"What's scata-whatsis mean?" Sandy whined.

"Look it up," said Alex.

"Since when did you ever obey anyone's rule, witchlette?" Gus wanted to know.

Angel shot him an offended look, then spoiled the effect by laughing, which sent Sandy off into a gale of giggles, and the moment passed.

"Oh, wow, this is fun," Sandy exclaimed, beaming around the scrubbed maple table. "Why don't we eat in here all the time?"

"In the first place, I don't think Mrs. Gilly would appreciate it. Not to mention that we'd be in Flora's way."

Somewhere in the house, a clock struck eleven, just as Angel did her best to cover a yawn.

"Are we keeping you up?" Alex inquired politely.

Sandy promptly took the blame. "I couldn't sleep last night, and Angel sat up with me and told me all these stories about when you were a little boy, Daddy. I never knew you were, like, um..."

"Like what? Like young? Like human?" He reached over and tugged a limp hank of pale blond hair. "I thought the doctor had given you some pills to help you get to sleep."

"Angel doesn't think I should take them."

In a moment of silence, the temperature dropped several degrees. "I wasn't aware that Angel had a license to practice medicine," Alex said in that controlled tone of voice that instantly shattered the party mood.

"If I goofed, I'm sorry. Sandy assured me she wasn't in great pain, and staying awake isn't going to hurt her ankle as long as she rests it. I just don't happen to approve of popping pills for every little ache and pain. It's a—'' Alex raked back his chair. "Gus, Sandy—will you excuse us, please?" He didn't precisely lift Angel out of her chair by her arm, but the effect was largely the same.

Sandy protested. When Gus placed a staying hand on her arm, she cried plaintively, "But why is he upset with Angel? She was only trying to help."

"Shh, don't sweat it, kid. Angel can hold her own." He only hoped it was true. Gus wasn't sure whether or not Alex was even aware of the unfair advantage he had where Angel was concerned.

Angel had heard of being frog-marched. Now she knew how it felt. When the marcher was six foot two, and the marchee was only five foot two, a helping hand under the elbow took on an entirely different meaning.

By the time they reached the study, she had stoked up a full head of steam. "Hightower, if you don't let go of my arm," she said with quiet sincerity, "I'm going to clobber you."

Alex released her abruptly. She staggered a few steps, rubbing her arm and searching his face for a clue. It would have helped if she could figure out what she'd said to set him off. One minute they'd all been laughing. The next moment it was bombs away.

"Well?" Crossing her arms over her chest, she began to pat one foot rapidly. Her warning rattle, Gus used to call it. Unfortunately, when one was barefoot and standing on a rug, the effect left a lot to be desired. While she waited, Alex began to pace. Oddly enough, the more he paced, the more her anger faded. "Alex, she's fine. The swelling's gone down a lot. I'm pretty sure no damage was done, but if you'd like, I'll pay for the doctor to—"

"I owe you an apology," he said quietly, knocking the wind right out of her sails.

Damn right, he did! Smugly she waited to hear it. "Well?" she prompted when it appeared as if that were all the apology she was going to get—the promise of one.

"Sorry." His bleak smile was almost worse than no smile at all. "You never really knew Dina, did you?"

"Your wife?" Angel was confused. She'd thought they were talking about Sandy—about her own countermanding the doctor's orders. Was he going to apologize after all these years for breaking her schoolgirl's heart by marrying that gold-plated bimbo?

"For some women, children are probably the chief raison d'être."

"They are? Look, would you mind speaking English? The only foreign language I know is a few Polish swearwords and some Latin plant names."

"Sorry."

That was her apology? Big deal.

"The thing is, Dina wasn't what anyone could call maternal. Sandy was born prematurely. She was sick a lot as a child. Dina had trouble finding a satisfactory nanny, so the poor kid ended up spending a lot of time in day-care, where she picked up everything going around. I guess they all do."

Angel nodded, wondering where this monologue was headed.

"She was especially prone to ear infections. Once they got started, they were the very devil to cure. We had drops to use both before and after she went in the water, but if those didn't work, it took antibiotics to knock it out.''

At the far end of the paneled room he braced his hands against the wall of books, and Angel stared at his back—the narrow hips, the long, tapered torso, the wide shoulders. He looked as if he might be in pain, which was crazy, because Sandy was the one with the sprained ankle.

Angel ached to go to him and offer whatever comfort she could, but she didn't dare. The Hightowers of this world had always been a touch above, and Alex was definitely above her touch.

''I was usually at work all day. Then, too, I traveled a lot in those days, and Dina . . . didn't always remember. Either the drops or the antibiotics. She assured me that earaches were a natural part of growing up, and like a fool, I believed her.''

His hands fell away from the shelves. He raked back his hair, and his bitter parody of a smile drew her across the room like a magnet. She wasn't conscious of having moved until he reached out and rested his arms across her shoulders.

If it wasn't an embrace, it was the next best thing. Angel closed her eyes and breathed in the essence of wool and starched cotton, of some crisp, light cologne, and the heady scent of warm male flesh.

''Dina was always popular.'' His voice was a soft rasp.

Forget Dina, she's gone. I'm here now.

''She had a lot of friends, and she enjoyed their company. Certainly she preferred it to spending her evenings with a sickly child and a dull stick of a husband." Again Angel caught a glimpse of that bleak smile. "But sometimes she forgot to leave instructions with the baby-sitter about Sandy's medicine, and I wasn't always there when I should have been to see that the doctor's instructions were carried out."

"But you worked. You traveled."

"True, but that's no excuse. Sandy should've been my first priority."

"Did Dina have a job?" Women like Dina Hightower didn't have jobs, they took positions.

Alex shook his head. His arms still rested heavily on her shoulders. For all his leanness, he was tall and big boned, yet she bore the weight joyfully. "She stayed pretty busy with charity auctions, bridge tournaments, committee work—you know the sort of thing."

Angel didn't. In the Reilly and Wydowski families, when a man had a job and a woman didn't work outside the home, it was his responsibility to support them, hers to look after the children. Which was pretty simplistic in this day and age, she'd be the first to admit. Even so...

"And that's why you got upset about Sandy's pain pills?"

He nodded, his forehead coming to rest on the top of her head, almost as if by accident. As if he were too tired to hold it up any longer. "I guess you could call it a knee-jerk reaction. Still, if Sandy doesn't think she needs them, who am I to say she does?"

He began idly toying with her hair, which was tied back with a ribbon. It always had to be restrained after her nightly hundred strokes. "Cal took pills for everything," she said, feeling a need to explain her position. "To speed him up, to slow him down—to make him feel good when he had every right to feel lousy. When he ran out of pills and we couldn't afford more, things could get pretty grisly. Sometimes he—"

Her lips tightened. The last thing Alex needed now was a recital of her own dismal marriage. Not even Gus knew the worst of it. She wondered if anyone who hadn't experienced it could understand what it was like to live with someone who existed on a different plane half the time.

And then he said, "Sandy has eighty percent hearing in her left ear, but only fifty percent in her right."

"Oh, no! I didn't realize . . ."

"It happened when she was three. I was in New York on business for nearly a week. Dina let the baby-sitter take her swimming at the club every day, but she forgot to instruct her to put in drops before and after. Before the baby-sitter realized what was wrong, an infection had set in."

"Oh, poor baby—the pain . . ."

"I'm afraid Dina wasn't as diligent with the antibiotics as she might have been, either." He would never forgive her for it. That had been the beginning of the end of their marriage. "By the time I got home, things were pretty rough."

What had been up until then a casual embrace— hardly an embrace at all—changed subtly as Angel slipped her arms around his waist, wanting to take away his hurt, his daughter's hurt, and bear it all on her own narrow shoulders. "Poor Sandy," she whispered. "Being fourteen is tough enough, without that."

"She covers well, but yeah—she's self-conscious. Sometimes I wonder if that's not the reason she wears all those god-awful earrings. Maybe she's subconsciously trying to call attention to her problem, trying to force the world to accept her as she is."

"I guess in a crazy sort of way, it makes sense. I never studied psychology."

Sharing burdens brought on an imperceptible lightening in the atmosphere. "What did you study, Angeline Wydowski? Forestry? Witchery?"

"You'll laugh."

"Try me."

She couldn't think of anything she'd rather do than try him, only she didn't think they had the same sort of trying in mind. "I was planning to go into politics, starting out small, like maybe city councilwoman, and working my way up to a state level, and maybe—well, who knows?"

"Good God," he said reverently. He was still holding her. She wondered if he'd forgotten where he'd left his arms.

"Only I got sidetracked. And anyway, I never got any further than my second year. College takes more time when you're working a couple of jobs."

She thought he sighed. At least he didn't offer any wisecracks about her choice of careers.

Several moments passed in silence. "Angel?" he murmured, and the low pitch of his voice set off tremors along every fault line in her body.

She tilted her head to stare up at him, still hanging on to his waist, trying to pretend she'd forgotten where she'd left her arms. ''What?'' she whispered, and her eyes went out of focus just as he lowered his mouth to hers.

Eight

On any seismograph in the world, the kiss would have registered a resounding eight. On Angel's personal meter, the conclusion was painfully clear. She was head over heels in love, and this time she was no impressionable teenager. This time she was an experienced woman who should have known better than to stray too close to the edge.

If she had spent practically her entire lifetime wondering what it would be like to kiss Alex Hightower—and she had—nothing she could have imagined would possibly have come close to the reality.

The taste of him—the incredibly intimate feel of his lips—the scent of his skin. How could something so soft be so firm?

When the tip of his tongue touched her own, she moaned, and as if the sound of that one small whimper drove him wild, he crushed her against his hard, straining body, his mouth grinding against hers as if he could never get enough of her.

His urgency was contagious, sparking back and forth between them like a newly exposed live wire. Catching bunches of shirt in her fists, she tugged, uncovering his back so that she could slide her hands over his naked skin.

He rolled his mouth over hers, his breath as ragged as her own. "This wasn't supposed to happen," he rasped, his breath hot on her face.

"Yes, it was." Her hands slid down the bunched muscles on either side of his spine, and she let gravity have its way with her. Her small palms slipped past his belt, and as they cupped his taut buttocks, she felt him surge against her. Her knees buckled. She might have fallen if he hadn't been holding her so tightly.

He was taller than she was. Squirming against him, she rose to her tiptoes. His arousal thrust aggressively against her belly, but that wasn't where she ached. She wanted him *there!*

She wanted him everywhere.

The subtle scent of a masculine cologne slipped into her consciousness—something warm and sensual and intensely personal. In the outer fringes of her mind, she was vaguely conscious of the background aroma of coffee, furniture polish and leather. The resulting blend was an incredibly intoxicating aphrodisiac.

As if she needed any help.

His lips lifted, brushing back and forth, moving slowly over hers so that she barely felt the pressure, only the heat and the sweet, dragging texture of moist skin on moist skin.

Her name on his lips, whispered over and over, was like a drug. *Oh, yes—yes, please!*

He kissed her a dozen times. Fierce, devastating kisses that drew her very soul from her body. Tiny, sweet candy kisses down her throat, behind her ears, that made her want to tear off her clothes so that he could go further. She whimpered, barely able to stand, and willed time to be still. Wished that before they both came tumbling down to earth again he would lower her to the carpeted floor and—

"*Da*-addy! Tell Gus I don't have to go back to bed right now!"

Alex's arms fell away. Stricken, he stared down at the small, flushed face, the swollen lips, the haunted eyes. "God, Angel, I'm s—"

"Don't you dare," she seethed, fighting tears of disappointment.

"Don't I dare what?"

"Apologize."

"*Daddy!* I know you're in there—why don't you answer me?"

Somehow, they got through the next few moments. They avoided looking at each other while Angel buttoned her top two buttons and smoothed her hair with unsteady fingers. His face totally without expression, Alex tucked his shirt back into his pants and then shook his head, as if he'd momentarily lost touch with reality.

It was Gus who carried Sandy to her bed while Alex locked up downstairs. Angel saw to getting the invalid settled for the night, avoiding her questions but unable to avoid her curious looks.

By that time, it was nearly midnight. Sandy yawned. Angel said, "I'm right across the hall if you need me. G'night, honey." She snapped off the light and slipped out the door just as Alex was coming upstairs.

They both stared. Neither of them spoke, but the tension between them was so great they might as well have hung up a banner, spelling out what was on both their minds.

Sex. In glowing, neon letters.

Angel had never wanted a man so much in her entire life, as she wanted this one. What's more, she was experienced enough to know that it was far from one-sided.

Unlike the first time she'd experienced such a tidal wave of sheer, physical wanting, when she'd stepped on a piece of broken glass that had cut through the side of her sandal and Alex had had to carry her to Gus's pickup truck, this time she was no adolescent. This time they were both adults. Neither one of them was committed to anyone else—at least she wasn't. So why not—?

We can't—not with Sandy sleeping across the hall and Gus two rooms down!

We can, too! Good Lord, woman, get real—this is the nineties! Women even have the vote now!

"Did you say something?" Alex asked.

"No. That is—did you?"

"No."

"Oh."

"Well . . . good night then, Angel."

Wistfully she wondered if that could possibly be taken as an endearment. Why couldn't she have been called Lina? Or Angie? Or just plain Ann? Anything but Angel. Now she'd never know.

At least he hadn't called her Devil, the way he used to when he wanted to tease her. "Good night, Alex."

"See you tomorrow."

She nodded, mentally crossing her fingers. This had gone far enough. She'd be a fool to hang around, waiting for any stray crumbs of affection he happened to toss her way—hoping against hope he would suddenly wake up and realize that he'd been in love with her for the past twenty years. If she had half a brain in her head, she would march right back to her side of town where she belonged. Back on her own turf, and on her own terms, she stood a chance, at least, of eventually working him out of her system.

Sandy would survive. If necessary, Alex could call on Carol. Or a nursing agency.

In any case, Angel had her own salvation to worry about. Only as it turned out, her salvation had to wait another day.

On his way downstairs just past seven on Monday morning, Gus rapped softly on Sandy's door. "Sandy? You awake yet?"

"Gus? Come in! I couldn't sleep a wink all night."

He stuck his head through the doorway. "I just wanted to say goodbye before I take off."

"Take off where? You said you weren't going right away."

"Sorry, hon. I got a call late last night that changes my schedule. Some unfinished business back in Banner Elk that'll have to be taken care of before I head east again. You take good care, y'hear? Maybe I'll drop in and see how you're getting along on my way east in a couple of weeks."

In the room across the hall, Angel heard the whispered conversation. Oh boy, what a way to start the day. Slipping into the hallway, she spoke briefly to her brother, and then braced herself to face Sandy and say her own goodbyes.

She might have known it wouldn't be that easy. Sandy was in no mood to be reasonable. She whined. She pouted. Angel felt like telling her to grow up, but she understood all too well that growing up wasn't something that could be done on command.

"You can't leave, too! What about me? I itch, and my ankle hurts too bad to go to school," Sandy wailed. "Gus promised me he'd stay awhile!"

"I think what he said was that he hoped he'd be able to stay a few days. That's hardly the same as promising."

"But I wanted him to take me to school today so everybody could see him. Reba and Debbie didn't believe me when I told them how awesome he was and about his beard and his truck and all."

"I'm sorry, Sandy, but—"

"Daddy, make her stay! Gus is gone, and now Angel says she has to go, too, and I'll be all alone up here, all by myself. What if I have to get up to go to the bathroom? I could fall down and break my neck, and nobody would even care!"

Alex had come up so silently Angel hadn't even realized he was there. After a largely sleepless night, she simply lacked the energy to fight. "All right, then, I'll stay and get you situated first, but then I have to go to work for a few hours."

"But you'll come back?" Sandy pleaded.

He was standing behind her in the doorway, so close she could feel the warmth of his body. One swift over-the-shoulder glance was enough to rock her senses. He was still in his pajamas, just as she was. In the soft early-morning sunlight filtering in through Sandy's white eyelet curtains, he looked good enough to eat with a spoon, all tousled and warm and tempting as chocolate-covered sin.

Knowing full well she needed her head examined, Angel heard herself promise to come back for lunch, and to spend one more night under the roof of the enemy. "Just one more night, Sandy, and that's final. Once you're on your feet again, Flora and Mrs. Gilly can cope."

"I'm only staying for your daughter's sake," she whispered fiercely to Alex the minute they were alone together in the upstairs hall.

His pajamas were gray silk, piped in some rich, dark paisley. She'd often wondered if he slept nude, or maybe in briefs, trying to imagine him both ways.

This was worse. The top hung from his shoulders and curved over his surprisingly powerful chest, while the bottoms, which were much narrower, skimmed down his lean flanks in a way that made her mouth go dry. Imagination was a much more powerful aphro-disiac than mere nudity.

"I just wanted to be sure you knew that my staying has nothing to do with what happened last night, be-cause we both know that it didn't mean anything. It—it just happened, that's all."

Alex continued to regard her with the cool steadi-ness that had always had the effect of gumming up her brain. The calmer he remained, the more agitated she grew. Some things never changed.

"She was disappointed about Gus, so I gave in, okay? But I'll be leaving right after breakfast tomorrow!" *Speak, damn you! Tell me you can't let me go. Tell me you can't live without me!* "It's only a sprain, for heaven's sake! It's not like she'll be bedridden for the rest of her life!"

"Thank you, Angel. I'm fully aware of the fact that you're staying only for Sandy's sake. I promise you, I won't take advantage of it."

"Yes, well . . . I'll be here tonight, but I'll be leaving first thing tomorrow morning for good, in case you need to make other arrangements."

Alex came downstairs some twenty minutes later wearing his newest suit and his favorite tie. He'd showered and shaved in record time, keeping an eye on her van through the window. It was still parked in the driveway, which meant she hadn't left yet.

They met in the breakfast room. Angel was wearing her coveralls, which were almost as bad as those damned red flannel pajamas that fit like a tent. The trouble was, it didn't seem to matter. Regardless of what she wore, she could turn him on like a light bulb.

God help him if he ever caught her in something sheer and clinging. He'd explode on the spot. Seven forty-five in the morning, he hadn't even had his coffee, and all he could think of was tearing off his clothes, planting her back on the table and burying himself so deep in her sweet little body he wouldn't surface again until the first snow began to fall.

He should never have brought her here. After last night he should have driven her home and then ordered up a practical nurse to do whatever needed doing.

"Good morning again," he said, steeling himself to behave like a staid, middle-aged businessman on his way to work instead of a wild, rutting stallion scenting a mare in heat. "Have you had br—"

His voice faltered as he stared down at the mess in his plate. "What the devil is this?"

"Breakfast. A sensible breakfast. I spoke to Flora about it yesterday, and you know what? I think that woman needs dosing with something. I never saw anyone with a sourer disposition. Anyway, I explained about the proper diet for a sedentary man, so from now on, you won't have to worry so much about cholesterol. I don't suppose you've ever had a weight problem, but a man your age can't be—"

That was when he exploded. Glaring first at the cool, self-righteous little female who had the audacity to meddle with his food, and then down at the mess on his plate, he began to swear. "What the hell happened to my sausage and fried eggs and hash browns?"

"I just told you."

"And what the hell business is it of yours what I eat, anyway? Has anyone ever told you that you're the bossiest female east of the Rockies?"

"As a matter of fact, yes, but I'm only trying to be helpful. If you recall, you're the one who brought me here. I didn't ask to come. I do have a life of my own, you know, but Sandy said last week that you acted like you hadn't been feeling good lately, so I promised her that while I was here I'd look into it."

"Oh, you did, did you?" His voice was quiet, reminding her of that old saw about the calm before the storm.

"Yes, well—I do happen to know something about—I mean, anyone who can read these days knows better than to dig their grave with a fork and spoon. The only exercise you ever get is sitting on top of a horse while he does all the work."

"And swimming. Don't forget swimming," he said in that same dangerous tone of voice.

"Yes, well . . . it's not a very big pool. And anyway, even if you weren't so uptight and didn't have that nasty temper, you'd still be at risk, with the way you eat. Steaks and cheeses and all those rich, buttery desserts. I haven't seen a salad since I've been here. For Sandy's sake, Alex, you really ought to take better care of yourself. Learn to relax. Lighten up. You'll last longer."

He was torn between the urge to strangle her and the equally powerful urge to make her a permanent part of his life. He resented her meddling. He resented the way she'd come barging back into his life again, reminding him of how guilty he used to feel because he lusted after a kid—his own best friend's sister—at a time when he was damned well old enough to know better.

He resented everything about Angel Wydowski. And yet, he had to admit that it had been a long time—a hell of a long time—since his health and well-being had mattered to anyone outside his insurance agency. It was a strange feeling, having someone care.

A feeling, he reminded himself, that he couldn't afford to grow accustomed to. "So what is this stuff, anyway?" He poked at the white lumpy blob on his plate.

"Omelet. It's made with egg whites instead of whole eggs, and filled with fresh vegetables and fat-free sour cream."

He closed his eyes. "Please tell me you're just joking."

"You'll get used to it in no time."

He sighed, resigned to his fate, and lifted his fork. At least it had distracted him from another problem—one that would be damned embarrassing if he weren't seated at the table. Egg whites and vegetables for breakfast, whole wheat toast and an apple, instead of real food topped off with a croissant slathered with creamery butter and strawberry jam.

"At least you didn't take away my coffee," he muttered, reaching for the large porcelain mug of rich, black, custom ground Columbian. "Thank God for small favors."

And then he gulped. His eyes grew round. Glaring at her, he snarled, "What the devil happened to my coffee? It tastes like ditch water!"

"It does not. The only thing that's been removed is the caffeine. You'll get used to it in no time."

And then she turned her attention to her own rich, black, custom-blended Columbian, and her own cheese omelet. With bacon. Angel had no health problems. Her cholesterol had never been above 166, her weight, if not its distribution, was just right for her height, and her blood pressure was an unfluctuating

118 over 68. Other than the usual childhood diseases, she had never been sick a day in her life.

Although, to be perfectly honest, her blood pressure might have done a few barrel rolls last night, while Alex had been kissing her senseless.

As good as her word, Angel spent that night at Alex's house, taking her supper on a tray in Sandy's room and going to bed shortly afterward. But she made certain everyone understood her position right from the first.

She had a life of her own.

She had a business to manage.

This was the second busiest time of the year for a landscape nursery, and besides, the longer she was exposed to Alex, the harder it was going to be to get on with the first two items.

Alex told himself it was better this way. All the blasted woman did was disrupt what had once been a perfectly orderly existence.

Or as orderly as any existence could be when it included a fourteen-and-a-half-year-old daughter, a housekeeper who couldn't climb stairs and who couldn't remember any instruction for more than half an hour, and a surly cook who had recently developed a sadistic streak.

There was certainly no point in getting used to a situation that wouldn't last. Besides, who needed some damned busybody telling him how to live and what to eat, and taking away the few pleasures he had left without offering anything in return?

Forget Angel Wydowski, he told himself, with the result that over the next few days, he managed to occupy himself with the buy-out and the fall furniture market to the extent that he seldom spent more than eight hours out of every twenty-four thinking about her.

What was it Gus used to call her? Witchlette?

She had sure as hell bewitched everyone in his household, with the possible exception of Flora. On her, she'd laid a fat-free curse.

Mrs. Gilly wanted to know if Ms. Perkins would be back in time for the fall turnover, because if not, she was going to need to hire someone.

A tradition begun by his mother, the biannual upheaval consisted of turning out the linen closet in search of yellowed linens, replacing slipcovers, counterpanes and draperies with something more suited to the coming season, swapping accessories—crystal for brass, fresh flowers for dried arrangements and evergreens and so on. In the process, everything got washed, waxed, polished and inventoried.

Then there was Mr. Gilly, who complained that Miz Angel had promised to help out with those blamed maples and thinning out the *Elaeagnus* and the bird's-nest spruce, and what about reseeding the front lawn? What about *that*, huh? And where was that blamed thatch-buster she'd promised him that he was supposed to shake up with Pepsi and spray on the lawn?

Unable to understand a single question, much less provide an answer, Alex retreated to his study, where he found Sandy, her long limbs twisted around the legs of a chair as she pored over what looked suspiciously like a romance novel.

"Studying?" he asked mildly.

"Um...I finished my homework early, so I thought I'd read this book Angel left behind. Angel says romance books are all about today's women facing up to today's problems, and boy, that sure describes me. This one's all about this woman who—"

Alex didn't want to hear what it was all about. He particularly didn't want to hear about Angel's ideas concerning romance. He had his own ideas, and they didn't include walking into the same trap twice.

It irritated the devil out of him that every other sentence from his daughter these days began with "Angel says—" or "Angel thinks—"

He didn't want to know what Angel said or Angel thought. He was doing his damnedest to put the woman out of his mind!

To be perfectly fair, however, he was forced to admit that under the Wydowski influence, he'd occasionally forgotten to treat his daughter like an alien life-form and begun to treat her as a human being. They'd even had several reasonably enjoyable, adult-type conversations that had nothing at all to do with Arvid Moncrief or clothes or curfews or homework.

It was just such an adult-type conversation that sent him racing across town a week later. He'd been talking to Carol on the phone, trying to explain why he couldn't get away from the office to drive her to Southern Pines for the weekend.

Sandy had been waiting to use the phone. Theirs was an old-fashioned household with only a single phone line.

Alex had hung up, irritated at having been made to feel guilty because he didn't want to spend an entire weekend playing golf and partying with Carol English. Sandy, interpreting his mood correctly but mistaking the cause of it, dialed a number and said, "Look, can you hang on a minute, Janet? I need to tell my dad something."

Clutching the phone to her chest, she said, "Daddy, you were pretty rough on Carol. You've been like, wow, you're mad at the whole world lately, so I've been doing some thinking about it. Like, I think I know what your trouble is."

"So you think I've overdosed on health food? You may be right, princess."

"No, I mean sex."

Sex?

"I mean, it's not like you're dead or anything."

Huh?

"I mean, sure, you're past your prime and all that, but my biology teacher says even old people need sex. It has something to do with—um, feeling close and all that junk? So if you don't want to do it with Carol, and boy, I can understand that, then maybe you ought to go cruising. I know some places where old guys hang out. They could prob'ly tell you where to find safe women."

Alex could actually feel his face turning purple. He managed to escape before he strangled, calling to Mrs. Gilly on his way out the door to tell her she was in charge until he got back.

Nine

Shocked right down to his toenails, Alex raced across town, swearing at red lights, nearly causing an accident when he passed a double-parked delivery van.

Old guys? How the hell did she know where old guys hung out?

He would wring her neck.

No, dammit, he would ground her for the next ten years, and then let her out only on a leash!

Cruising?

Oh, God.

Yeah, but safe women? If she meant what he thought she meant, then maybe she still had one or two functioning gray cells under all that butter-colored hair.

The area in front of Angel's establishment that had so recently been ruined by tons of water and a fleet of heavy fire trucks had now been graded and regraveled. Alex roared in through the open gate, displacing a few yards of gravel as he swerved over to the far side.

"Angel!" he roared before both feet had even hit the ground. "Get on out here! This is an emergency!"

Half in and half out of the old claw-footed bathtub, Angel craned her neck toward the small, badly placed window that looked out on the side yard. She could have sworn she heard Alex's voice.

But then, she'd been hearing his voice, not to mention seeing his face, ever since she'd moved back home. She had tried her darnedest to relive his kiss again, but how does one relive a taste?

She heard the front doorbell ring and tried to remember whether or not she had locked it.

She hadn't. She'd been functioning with half a brain for so long now, it was a wonder she hadn't locked herself out.

"Angel? Where the devil are you?" She heard his footsteps cross the pine floor in the living room, the vinyl in the kitchen.

He wouldn't.

"I know you're in here somewhere, because your van's parked outside and the greenhouse is locked."

Oh, fine. She remembered to lock the greenhouse but forgot to lock her own front door. It figured.

She heard the back door hinges squeak, hopped out of the tub and lunged for the bathrobe hanging on the back of the door just as the door swung in.

Lunged and missed.

The towel was on the opposite wall. There was no shower curtain, because when you had a window right over the middle of the darned bathtub, you could hardly have a shower, could you? And besides, she preferred long, hot soaks—even in the summertime.

Alex stared. His mouth opened once or twice, but no sound issued forth. His eyes moved slowly over her dripping wet body—the broad hips, vestigial breasts, callused, bandaged thumb, where she'd worn a hole in her work gloves and gone right on working—sun-blistered nose where she'd forgotten to smear on a layer of SPF 30, and all.

"I—I'm sorry," he whispered.

"*You're* sorry!" Angel was sorry, too. Sorry he hadn't caught her lying on the sofa, peeling a grape, wearing something wispy and expensive and seductive—something that hinted at hidden treasures while, at the same time, disguising certain shortcomings. "Would you mind giving me my bathrobe from behind the door and then getting the hell out of here?"

He fumbled behind the door for the faded old striped bathrobe that had belonged to Cal's father. They had bought it for him after he'd had his heart attack, but he'd never worn it, and Cal hadn't liked robes, so Angel had fallen heir to the thing.

Waste not, want not.

"I need to talk to you."

"Then wait in the living room."

"Where—"

"Across the porch, through the kitchen, and you're in it. I only have five rooms, for heaven's sake! Now, get out!"

Alex got, carrying with him the indelible image of a small, incredibly female figure, her small, milk-white breasts tipped with brown puckered nipples that excited him more than any breast he could remember since he'd seen his first one at the impressionable age of thirteen.

As for the thatch of dark russet hair nestled at the apex of a pair of sweetly rounded thighs...

He swallowed hard, feeling something akin to panic.

He had come here because...

Why the hell had he come here, anyway? To seduce her? To convince her to come home with him again?

Oboy. He was too old for this kind of thing. There'd been a time in his life when he'd been led around by his gonads. Most guys between the ages of eighteen and twenty-five were. It had something to do with nature's determination to propagate the species, come hell or high water.

Only this was different. He was years past his sexual prime, if the experts could be believed—not that he put much stock in the kind of self-styled experts that spouted off at the drop of a hat simply to justify some grant or other. And anyway, the last thing on his mind was propagation of any sort. All he wanted was plain, old-fashioned sex.

All he wanted was Angel.

"Now. What was so all-fired important that you had to break into my house to tell me?"

At the sound of her voice, he spun around, guilt written all over his bony, patrician features. She was standing in the doorway, arms crossed over her chest, that foot of hers going like an air-hammer.

"It's Sandy."

The foot stilled. The arms fell to her sides. "What's she done now? Is she all right? For heaven's sake, tell me, don't just stand there!"

"She's all right," he managed to say. He was losing it, Alex decided. It was bad enough that she could punch his buttons wearing red flannel pajamas or a pair of shapeless green coveralls with a name patch on the front and Perkins Landscaping & Nursery scrawled in acid green on the back.

In a brown-and-white seersucker bathrobe that was at least ten sizes too large, she was lethal. The thing lapped around her twice, and still gaped open down the front, too close to the danger zone for comfort.

His comfort, at least. He was fully aroused and there wasn't one damned thing he could do about it. Except try to keep her eyes above his belt until he could manage to bring himself under control.

"Down, boy," he murmured.

"What?"

"I said—" God, he was actually blushing! "It's Sandy—she's got me really worried this time, Angel. I, um—I want you to talk to her. Please?"

She dropped down onto a rocking chair that looked as if it had racked up about a hundred thousand miles. One bare foot lapped earnestly over the other and the robe fell open over her knees.

She had a bandage on her knee, too.

"What is it this time—Arvid?"

"Who?"

"Kid Corvette."

"Oh. No, it's, uh—it's me."

Angel set the chair into motion. She'd found it helped drain nervous tension away when she had a problem. And boy, did she evermore have a problem!

Alex was careful to keep Mrs. Perkins's precious velvet love seat between them, but Angel was no fool. She'd seen the condition he was in right off. The truth was, she was in pretty much the same shape, only women had the advantage over men. She could play it cool, and he'd never even suspect.

"So—what's up?" she quipped brightly.

I didn't say that, I didn't, I didn't, I didn't.

He leaned over the back of the love seat, bracing his arms on the rosewood carving, and stared down at the newspaper she'd left open to the comics.

Oh, for pity's sake, why the comics? Why couldn't she have left it open to the editorial page?

"Like I said, it's Sandy."

"You said it was you."

"Yes, well—in a manner of speaking."

"Look, do you want to tell me what's wrong, or don't you? I mean, I *do* have other things to do."

He looked stricken. "You've got a date?"

She would dearly love to lie and say she had, only she'd never been any good at it. Her skin was too thin. She turned red, and her eyes, according to Gus, got glassy, so she'd learned to tell the truth and suffer the consequences.

"I had planned to start peeling off the wallpaper in my bedroom. It smells of smoke, and it's at least two shades darker since the fire."

"She said if I need sex, I should go cruising."

Now it was Angel's turn to gape.

"She also said she knows of a place where a lot of old guys hang out, who might be able to help me find—I think her words were—'safe women.' Could someone please tell me what the hell goes on with kids these days?"

Angel took a moment to digest the problem, and then said calmly, "Not a whole lot that didn't always go on, I reckon. Only more of it. In some quarters, at least."

"Not in my quarters!"

"Yes, well—I didn't think so."

"You mean you think she's just blowing off?"

"I'm not sure, I just said I didn't think so. What brought up the subject, anyway?"

"My disposition." He could have done without her knowing grin.

"Well, don't blame me. I did all I could to help fix what ailed you."

"You did *what?*" She *was* what ailed him, didn't the fool woman even realize it?

"Didn't I tell you that along with a low-fat, high-fiber, low-caffeine diet, you need to exercise more? Sitting behind a desk all day—"

"Let's leave my unhealthy life-style out of this, shall we?" For a minute there, he'd thought she was talking about something else entirely. Something he knew damned well she had done nothing but exacerbate.

"If you insist, but even you ought to realize that if you wore yourself out physically, you wouldn't explode so often."

"Even me? I? What the hell does that mean?"

"Just what you think it means. Look at you, you're ready to explode, and we're only having a simple conversation, not even an argument. Didn't you ever read about geology? Plate tectonics, gas rings, volcanos and stuff like that? It's all about pressure, you know. Hidden pressures that search out hidden weaknesses, and then, ka-*boom!*"

"That does it," he said flatly, coming out from behind the love seat.

Angel rose and adjusted the folds of her voluminous bathrobe. "Good. I'm glad I was able to help out."

She lifted her gaze to his face and stepped back uncertainly. "Alex—?"

He moved forward, stalking her as surely as if he were a hungry lion and she were a skittish lamb. "Alex!"

Sandy had been right, he told himself. What he needed was sex. It had been—God, it had been years! The trouble was, he didn't want sex with just any woman, he wanted sex with Angel Wydowski. The same Angel Wydowski he had lusted after so guiltily twenty years ago.

"Stop backing away from me, dammit, I won't hurt you," he said. "I'm not going to do anything you don't want me to do, but Angel—you have to tell me."

"Tell you what?" she whispered helplessly.

"That you don't want me. That you want me to leave. That you—"

"Alex?"

"What."

"Shut up," she said softly, stepping forward an instant before he opened his arms.

Somehow, they made it as far as her bedroom, with the smoky wallpaper and the ivory-painted iron bed that had belonged to Aunt Zee. Angel had gotten rid of most of the original furniture in the house after Cal had been killed. Yard-saled all but a few pieces and then brought in the few things she had saved from her own family.

Now she was glad she had. Practically all her life she had wanted Alex Hightower, but she could never have made love to him in the same bed she'd slept in with Cal.

"You're sure?" he whispered, his hands and his voice unsteady as he ripped off his shirt.

"I'm sure." She was sure she was probably going to be sorry, but she'd be even sorrier if she'd had the chance and hadn't taken it.

She was sure she would never love another man, but that was her problem, not his. Alex tolerated her. He even liked her—when he wasn't furious with her. He definitely desired her.

Sometimes, she mused—on rare, Camelot occasions—Cinderellas who wore combat boots really did get the charming prince. If only for a little while.

She tugged at the sash that held her robe together, flushed with a feeling of something more heady than triumph. She was finally going to know what it was like to make love with Alex Hightower.

"Angel—I didn't bring anything. Are you, uh—are you protected?"

She turned off the light, leaving only the greenish glow from her security light outside, and told a bald-faced lie. "Don't worry about it, everything's taken care of."

But in a way, she rationalized, it truly was. This was her safe period, and besides, she'd never managed to conceive with Cal. She had wanted a baby. He hadn't.

As for any other risks, there'd been no one for her since her marriage had ended. Since several months before her marriage had ended, in fact, and she'd gone in for tests the day she'd first learned that Cal had been sleeping around.

As for Alex, he'd always been fastidious. It was only one of the things about him that appealed to her. He was the exact opposite of Cal.

"Oh, my," she breathed as he stepped out of his slacks and briefs in one motion and stood before her in all his naked splendor.

And splendid he was. Oh, my, yes. She had seen him in bathing trunks and in tennis shorts. She was prepared for the sight of his surprisingly wide shoulders, the broad chest dusted with dark hair, the narrow hips and long, muscular legs.

Her eyes skimmed appreciatively over all that and homed in on the other.

"Oh, my," she whispered again as her bathrobe crumpled soundlessly about her bare feet.

Embarrassed, she gestured awkwardly to the bed. "Do you—that is, shall we—?"

"Sure, why not?"

Smooth, Hightower. Really smooth.

Alex hardly recognized his own voice. He was trembling! If he lost control now, he'd never be able to face her again. With an unsteady hand, he turned back the covers. What was that she'd said about pressure? He was under so much pressure right now he was aching, and there was only one type of exercise that would cure it.

Ka-*boom!*

She slid into bed and pulled the covers up to her chin, and it occurred to him for the first time that in some ways she was still as self-conscious as she'd been as a kid.

But then, so was he. Where she was concerned. For reasons he didn't dare dwell on, it was important that he do this right, make it memorable for both of them. Maybe then, he wouldn't walk away with that old empty feeling that sex had always left him with. That was part of the reason he'd avoided it for so long. The depression that settled in afterward. The feeling that something vital was missing.

He came down beside her and wrestled her briefly for the covers. "Don't tell me you're nervous?"

"Of course I'm not," she denied too quickly. "Yes, I am, too."

"So am I. Kind of silly, isn't it, at our age?"

But neither of them felt like laughing. All Alex wanted to do was fold back the covers and turn on the overhead light and look his fill. And then he wanted to touch her everywhere and see how she felt, sample the texture of her skin with his hands, his lips—savor the taste of her on his tongue, and then, when he couldn't hold off another instant, he wanted to put himself inside her and die there, while she shouted his name and her hot little body convulsed all around him.

"You could kiss me again. That's always a good way to start," she suggested, and he began to chuckle.

"Are you telling me you're an expert on this, too?"

With a lopsided little grin, she said, "I'm in the nursery business, remember? Propagating is propagating."

"Don't even think it," he growled, but as he leaned over to bury his face in her sweet, soap-scented throat, he pictured a small, redheaded Hightower, ruling his roost with that go-to-hell charm that had always been a mark of the Wydowskis.

From her left ear, he kissed his way down her throat, down the gentle slope of her breast, until he found what he was seeking.

She shuddered and squirmed. She reached for him, her firm, capable little hands working their way down his body, driving him wild.

"Careful there—" His breath was coming in shivery gasps between his teeth.

But Angel didn't want to be careful, she wanted everything, all at once, on and on, with no end. And she wanted it now. Arching her back, she offered him her breasts, not even embarrassed because they were so very small. He made her feel beautiful. He made her feel as if she could fly!

"Ah, sweet, sweet Angel," he rasped against the flat of her belly. "You don't know how long I've dreamed about this." He nuzzled her navel, causing her whole body to stiffen.

Pillow talk, she told herself. Pillow talk doesn't count, it can't be held against either party.

I love you, I love you, I— "Oh, Alex—please!"

He moved over her then and hovered, gazing down at her with passion-glazed eyes. A film of moisture covered his body, making it gleam in the eerie light. Slowly, almost as if he were afraid of hurting her, he came into her, and for one brief, delirious moment, she possessed him completely, body and soul.

Slowly, tentatively, he began to thrust, and she met him halfway. More than halfway. As the sweet, mystical tension began to build, began to sing, they moved faster, racing to meet it headlong. Just when she thought she would die, he slipped his hand down and found her, and she hurled over the edge, shuddering, crying out, clinging to the only thing in the world that mattered.

Aware even then that he was shuddering, crying out and clinging, too.

She awoke in his arms in the dim green light that filtered through the window, not even wondering at the strangeness of finding herself not alone. She had dreamed of this so many times, it was more real in a way than reality.

Which was crazy, and probably a little bit dangerous, but she thought she would just indulge herself for a little while longer.

At least, she did until the phone began to ring.

"It's probably for you," she murmured drowsily. "I never get calls in the middle of the night."

"Me, either. Maybe it's a wrong number."

"Prob'ly." She moved her head on his chest so that her lips nuzzled his flat brown nipple. It peaked immediately, which caused all sorts of interesting chain reactions to take place.

The phone finally stopped ringing. In the long silence that followed, she began to trace the fault line that ran down from the small hollow where his neck joined his shoulder, across his nipple, circling his navel, leading directly to the danger zone. The area of greatest weakness. The volcanic region.

"You're asking for trouble," he whispered hoarsely. But he continued to lie there, arms over his head, allowing her full freedom to explore to her heart's content.

"Are you going to give me any?" she taunted, enjoying the flush that had crept over the sharp contours of his cheekbones.

"Trouble?"

"Whatever."

Lazily he rolled over, capturing her hand and nibbling his way up to her shoulder. "I might consider offering you a bit more whatever. You say you're an experienced rider?"

"Not very," she admitted, remembering the small lie she'd told. "But I'm a quick study."

His eyes strangely darkened under half-closed lids, he lifted her and swung her over him just as the phone started to ring again. "Damn." His eyes snapped open again. "Maybe you'd better get it, sweetheart. And leave it off the hook. This is one ride I don't want interrupted."

Reluctantly Angel climbed out of bed, swooping up her bathrobe along the way. He had seen everything there was to see. He knew she was hippy and flat chested. He knew her thighs were too plump, and her hair looked like a haystack after a windstorm, but there was no point in flaunting it.

She reached the phone just as the dial tone came on. "Damn, damn, damn," she swore softly, but not quite softly enough.

Alex joined her, stark, distractingly naked. "Who was it? Crank call?"

"Probably. Evidently there's a nut out there who thinks it's funny to get someone out of bed and then hang up just as they pick up the phone, and my answering machine is on the blink."

"Leave it off the hook."

"But what if it's not a crank call? Gus might be trying to reach me on his car phone. If he's headed down the mountains, he might go in and out of range, which would explain—"

"Take it off the hook. Five minutes won't matter."

"Why five minutes? You think that will discourage him?"

Standing just behind her, Alex slid his arms around her and buried his face in her neck, inhaling the intoxicating scent of sex and soap and the spicy-grassy smell that he'd come to recognize as hers alone.

"Because I need you again," he said in a voice that was suddenly hoarse with urgency. "Because I doubt if I can last more than five minutes. Something to do with all that pressure you were talking about earlier."

Turning her in his arms, he lowered his face just as she lifted hers. He was hard and ready, and she groaned softly. "I'm melting from the inside out," she whispered.

He slid her robe from her shoulders as she reached behind her to lift the phone off the hook. "If it's important—" She broke off with another soft groan as she felt him thrusting against her belly.

"They'll call back," he finished, his hands cupping her breasts, glorying in their delicacy, their sensitivity as she peaked hard under his fingertips.

"Put your arms around my neck, Angel." He slid his hands down under her thighs. "Hold on tight."

"Like this?" She stared into his eyes as he lifted her, sliding her up his body, spreading her thighs so that they embraced his ribs. And then he lowered her slowly.

This time it was Alex who groaned.

Angel gasped.

Two minutes, forty-seven seconds, not that anyone was keeping time.

Ka-*boom!*

Ten

———

Sandy was waiting for Alex when he returned home. He felt rumpled. He was certain it was obvious what he'd been doing, and only hoped she was still too innocent to guess.

"Well? Where is she?" she demanded. She had been sitting halfway down the stairs with a clear view of the front door, a stack of comic books, a chocolate milk carton and an empty cereal bowl beside her.

"What are you talking about? And what are you doing still up? Have you done your—"

"How could I concentrate on homework, when you go running off like that? Daddy, I worry about you! You don't seem to realize it, but you're at a dangerous age. My gym teacher says a lot of men go bonkers once they realize they're getting old, and—"

"Dammit, I am not getting old!" he roared. "And what the devil does that have to do with your homework, anyway?"

"So where's Angel? That's where you went, right? To talk to her about me? Did you do sex with her? Are you two going to get married? Because if you are, and you want some privacy, I can move to Grandma's sewing room downstairs. Nobody ever uses it anymore, and—"

But Alex had stopped listening. He didn't believe in spanking, although he would confess to having been tempted a time or two. A harsh word added to her own guilty conscience had usually been enough to do the trick.

At least it had been before his child had turned into a smart-mouthed pseudoadult before his very eyes.

He went for the glare. Thanks mostly to an accident of birth—pale hair, cool gray eyes and thick, level, near-black brows—his glare should have been enough to quell a riot.

Only lately, the glare hadn't worked, either.

She smirked at him. He felt a pulse begin to pound near his temple. "What makes you think I've been with Angel?"

"Because that's why I—well, like, I mean, you were, weren't you? I mean, it's no big deal. Like, I know you guys talk about me, because of some of the stuff Angel said when she was here, so I thought—" A look of horror suddenly crossed her face. "Daddy! You didn't go running off to see Carol, did you?"

With a tired sigh, Alex rubbed the back of his neck and flopped down onto the bottom step. He didn't want to have this conversation, but if she was determined to talk, he might as well let her get it off her chest. That was what fathers were for, right? For daughters to confide in.

Ha!

"I spoke to Angel. I told her you were worried about me, and she reminded me that a decent diet and a regular program of exercise—"

"Sure, but like, what about sex?"

"Dammit, Sandy, quit talking like that! All right, so maybe you do have a legitimate interest in my health. But my private life is none of your business, okay?"

"Okay. But if your sex life isn't any of my business, then mine isn't any of yours."

Alex shot to his feet, so scared that, for once, he even forgot to glare. "You're not—Sandy, tell me you're not—no, I don't want to hear this." He swore softly and paced a tight circle on the faded old rug. Pausing at the foot of the stairway, he gazed up at his young daughter, wondering when the child he'd taught to swim, taught to ride, taught to say "please" when she begged him for just one more story before bedtime, had turned into a stranger.

"Well, like, I mean, even if I had—"

"Please don't preface your statements with well-like-I mean," he said automatically, and could have kicked himself.

"Whatever. I mean, I—I mean, even if I had, you don't have to worry about me, Daddy, because I already know everything. I mean, my sex ed teacher is real cool. Like, she told us about all this really grotty stuff you have to do to keep from getting sick or pregnant?"

I don't want to hear this, God. Please let me wake up and find out it's all a dream.

"So, did you do it with Angel?"

"Alexandra!"

"Well, are you two going to get married, or what? Why didn't you bring her home with you? It wouldn't take her all that long to drive to work from here, and anyway, once you two are married, she'll probably stop working. I mean, Mama did, didn't she?"

"Your mother never worked a day in her life."

"She didn't? Well, like, whatever she did before you guys got married, she probably quit doing it once she was your wife, right?"

Wrong. That was part of why they had broken up. Dina hadn't allowed a small thing like a family—a husband and a daughter—to affect her preferred lifestyle. If Sandy hadn't turned out to look so much like the Hightowers, he might even have wondered . . .

But she had. Not that wondering would have changed the way he felt about her. He'd fallen head over heels in love with a bald-headed mite the first time she'd thrown up all over his shoulder and then stared up at him with those big, blurry blue eyes that had turned gray within weeks.

She'd been nearly three when Dina had left them both to fly up to New York to do her Christmas shopping. The next time he'd heard from her, it had been through her lawyer.

Sandy had been tearful for weeks afterward, but Dina had never been a hands-on parent, preferring to leave the nitty-gritty to a series of nannies and baby-sitters, and to Alex.

Feeling as if he'd been handed a live hand grenade, he had finally come up with a story the night of her third birthday party, when she'd kept watching the door, obviously waiting for someone, and then pitched a tantrum when the party ended with no sign of her mother.

She had cried herself sick. Alex had soothed her and bathed her and put her to bed. He had told her a tale about a beautiful mother who had gone away to become a princess, like the one in her favorite storybook, but because this princess's kingdom was so very, very far away, there was no way she could take her baby princess with her, even though she loved her very much and would always love her.

Yeah. Right.

"Why don't we both turn in, honey," he said now. "I'm really beat. We can talk some more tomorrow if you want to."

"We won't. You have to go to work tomorrow, just like you always do."

"And you have to go to school, but we'll make time, sweetheart, I promise."

Only they didn't talk. Just like he hadn't talked to Angel. Things were getting out of hand. He desperately needed help, only whenever he got near the one woman who seemed to have a grasp of what the problem was all about, he lost the whole damn ball of wax!

He was at work when Mrs. Gilly called him the next day. Right in the middle of a high-level conference, his secretary came in and waggled two fingers, their sign that something extremely urgent had come up, requiring his personal attention.

"I'm sorry, Mr. Hightower," she said after he turned matters over to his second in command, "It's your housekeeper, and she sounds really upset. She says you'd better go home right now."

Flowers. Someone—it could only have been Sandy—had cut out every blossom on her bedspread and arranged them in groups on the carpet in front of every piece of furniture in the room.

"What the hell—has she lost her mind?" Alex demanded.

"This is the way I found it," said Mrs. Gilly. She had insisted on hobbling up the stairs again, in spite of her knees. "She got this phone call from that Moncrief boy, only when I called her to pick up, she didn't answer, and I knew she was up here—that is, the last time I saw her she was. She came up directly after school, only then I remembered when I stepped out back to call Phil to come take his blood pressure medicine, I thought I heard the front door. I didn't think nothing of it at the time, because you know how— well, at any rate, when I called up the stairs for her to get the phone and she didn't answer, something didn't quite set right, so I come up here and this is what I found. I started to call Miss Angel, but then I decided I'd better call you first. I declare, Mr. Alex, I never seen anything like it in all my born days. Do you think—?"

He didn't think. He couldn't think. He was hurting, he was mad, and he was scared to death. "Why the devil would you call Angel?" he demanded.

The old woman twisted her gnarled fingers, making him regret his harsh tone. The Gillys had been a part of the Hightower household since long before his parents had died. They were family. "I'm sorry, Louella, I didn't mean that. I know you're as worried as I am, but I expect she's just playing a prank. Trying to get my attention. I promised her we'd talk, only I got tied up at the office, and..."

She patted his hand. "A prank, that's what it is. I only thought Miss Angel might know if something was bothering her, them being such good friends and all. A baby needs a mother, not that Miss Angel is really her—"

"Don't start on me, Mrs. Gilly. I don't need another wife, and Sandy's managed to get along all this time without a mother."

"Still and all, a friend, a woman she could talk to..."

"She has you if she needs to talk to a woman."

"Now, you know as good as I do, Mr. Alex, that there's nothing I wouldn't do for that young'un, but when it comes to talking the way folks does these days, why I wouldn't even know where to start. In my day—"

She was right, of course. Alex had heard enough about Louella Gilly's day to realize that there was a vast language gap, not to mention a couple of generations. He draped an arm over the old woman's shoulder and turned her toward the stairs. "You go on down and tell Phil that everything's under control," he said gently. "Then brew us up a pot of tea and maybe another one of coffee, if you don't mind."

As soon as the housekeeper had made her painful way down the curving stairway, he turned to the phone and quickly punched out a number.

"Landscaping. She's done the beds exactly the way—" Angel walked around the arrangement of lavender, blue and yellow blotches that spread out in front of the dresser, gnawing her lower lip. She had come the moment she'd gotten the call, not bothering to change out of her coveralls and the ratty old yellow turtleneck she wore under them. Her hair was wild, as usual, and she'd forgotten the pencil she'd shoved through her topknot earlier that day.

Thoughtfully she studied the patterns on the floor. "Of course, she didn't have anything to use for shrubbery."

"What the devil are you talking about? She's whacked up her damned bedspread! In my book, that's the mark of a disturbed mind."

"Not necessarily." Angel propped one elbow in her palm and rested her chin on the other fist. Flower beds. Sandy had tried her hand at planning flower beds using potted seedlings, Angel remembered now. She'd called Gus in to admire her efforts.

"I'm going to call the police. I was going to call them earlier, but I thought she might have gone off to your place."

"Wait. Just be quiet and let me think, will you?"

"Ah, hell, it's my fault," he said then, his voice rough with pain and worry. "If I hadn't overreacted—if I hadn't gone racing off after you last night and then—"

"And then wasted so much time in my bed."

"I didn't say that."

"You didn't have to. But Alex, this is not your fault. Whatever you did or didn't do, Sandy's a smart girl. She knows better than to go chasing off in the middle of the night without telling anyone, unless there's a very good reason.''

"It's three forty-seven in the afternoon.''

"You know what I mean. Alex, she's just trying to tell you something, that's all. She'll probably call up in a little while and ask if you got the message.''

"Message! If this is a message, it's a sick one! You can hang around up here and look at this—this desecration—as long as you want to. I'm going after the Moncrief brat and if she's not there, I'm going to pull a few teeth until I find out what the hell is going on!''

She didn't bother to argue. Sandy wouldn't be with Arvid, because Angel knew for a fact that whatever attraction the boy had held for her had already lost its potency. Which meant that after he'd thrown his weight around, Alex would call the police, and they would say the usual things to him that policemen said when a teenage girl left home without telling anyone in broad daylight, and was missing for a few hours.

What else could they say? She was probably at the mall shopping, or hanging out with a friend. Or simply staying out of sight to worry her father—to get across whatever point she was trying to get across.

Although, any possible point a whacked-up bedspread could make escaped her, it surely did.

The child was up to something...but what?

She heard Alex's car screech down the driveway. Thank goodness the Moncriefs lived in the neighborhood, because in his condition, he would be a definite traffic hazard. Turning her attention to Sandy's closet, Angel tried to recall every item they had pulled out and discussed one night when they'd come up to pick out a party outfit. She went over it once, and then went over it again, trying to remember, but there was so much, it would be impossible to say if anything was missing.

Ten minutes after he'd gone roaring off, she heard Alex come racing back. The car door slammed. The front door slammed, and then there was silence.

Obviously things hadn't gone too well at the Moncriefs' place.

Angel resumed her search for evidence. Or rather, for missing evidence. Her new earrings?

She was probably wearing those.

Hairbrush? Toothbrush? Makeup?

It was right there in all the clutter on her dressing table, between a bottle of frosted pink nail polish and a stack of photos, propped up on a ratty-looking pompom in the school's green and gold colors. She stared at the envelope for fully thirty seconds before she reached for it. If it'd been a snake...

It was addressed to Daddy. It was sealed. Angel was afraid to read it, afraid not to. Feeling suddenly cold, she picked it up and started to rip it open, then changed her mind.

By the time she found him in the study, Angel's hands were clammy and her mind had turned over roughly a zillion possibilities, none of them good.

A sealed note meant she probably hadn't just gone shopping. She'd have told Mrs. Gilly if that was all she had in mind. Or left a note on the refrigerator under a magnet.

A note addressed to Daddy, sealed in an envelope, meant she really had run off. But why on earth would she chop up a perfectly good Laura Ashley bedspread first?

"Alex," she said from the doorway, trying to sound calm and levelheaded, which was the very last thing she was feeling. "I found a note."

Sprawled in the big leather chair in his study, the telephone on the floor beside him, Alex was staring at the untouched drink in his hands, his eyes shadowed with worry. Evidently he hadn't found her at Arvid's house and was steeling himself to call the police.

He looked up when she spoke, and seeing the sudden flare of hope in his eyes, Angel felt like cradling him in her arms and promising that nothing would ever hurt him again.

But no one could promise that. Life was full of sharp edges.

"A note?" he asked warily. "What does it say?"

"I didn't open it. It's addressed to you." She wondered if Dina had done it this way. Run off with no notice, leaving a note on her dresser.

She handed him the envelope decorated with a childish design of flowers and unicorns, and he held it, staring down at it as if it might conceal an asp. "Open it," she said.

He handed it back. "Would you—?"

She would have bled for him if she could, but she was afraid no one could spare him the pain he was feeling now. Or the even greater pain he might be feeling in a moment.

Swallowing the thick lump in her throat, she ripped open the envelope and unfolded the single sheet of unicorn-decorated paper, scanning the few lines written in a childish hand. Then, dropping into the nearest chair, she leaned her head back and closed her eyes.

"Oh, God, that meddling little wretch!" she whispered.

The last vestige of color instantly drained from Alex's face. He lunged for the note. Angel wanted to tear it into small pieces, to burn it, to swallow it—anything to keep him from seeing it, but of course, he had to know.

"'Dear Daddy,'" he mumbled, reading aloud. "'By the time you read this I'll be staying with A Friend, so don't worry about me, I'm fine. You and Angel can have some privacy to work things out. You know what I mean.'"

"What does she mean?" Angel asked. "What do we have to work out?" And then her eyes grew round. "Alex, you didn't tell her—"

"That we—? Oh, hell, no! What kind of a man do you think I am?"

"Then why did she say that about privacy? Why does she think we need privacy? And what do we have to work out? And why was she so sure you'd know what she meant? Do you?"

Alex felt his face begin to burn in spite of the cold sweat that covered his body. "Yes, well . . . but what I can't figure out is why she thought she had to chop up a perfectly good bedspread."

"To get your attention, maybe? With a mule, it takes a two-by-four, but with fathers . . ."

Mrs. Gilly brought in a tray with coffee things and one of Flora's dry, grainy cakes, sliced and arranged on a Wedgwood plate. Alex nodded to Angel, and she poured from the heavy silver pot, remembering the only time she had served Alex coffee at her house.

Actually, he had served himself, directly from the coffee maker.

Alex told Mrs. Gilly about the note, and the woman promptly burst into tears and rushed out to tell her husband, who had just broached a new bottle of Thunderbird to help him cope with the emergency.

"What did you find at the Moncriefs'?"

"Arvid has strep throat."

"He *what?*"

"He called to warn her. I don't even want to know why."

"Did you call the police?"

He nodded. "So? What did they say?"

His smile held nothing of amusement. "Just what you thought they'd say. Check with her friends, wait at least twenty-four hours, chances are we'll hear from her before then."

Angel reached for the note and read it again, aware of his steady regard. After several endless minutes had ticked past, she decided that action—any action at all—was better than simply waiting. Especially when they didn't know what they were waiting for.

At least, Alex might, but she certainly didn't. All she knew—and actually, it was only a suspicion—was that it had something to do with her. "So, shall we start calling around to her friends?"

It was as if he had to pull himself back from some distant place. He hadn't touched his coffee. Neither of them had touched Flora's awful cake. The woman could ruin cake from a mix.

"Do you know if she had an address book?" Angel persisted.

"No—yes. That is, did you look in her desk drawer?"

She hadn't. She'd checked the closet and then the dresser, and once she'd found the note, she'd rushed downstairs. "I'll go check now."

Angel found the address book and they went through it systematically, saying the same lines each time, trying to sound as if they weren't half out of their minds. "May I please speak to Sandy Hightower? Oh, she's not there? I'm sorry, I must have misunderstood her. She said she was going over to study with a friend, and I thought—yes—no—thanks, sorry for bothering you."

Alex made the first half-dozen calls. Angel took over when she noticed the way his hands were shaking. "She's all right, Alex. She's with a friend, even if we don't know yet which one."

"Yeah," he growled. "How many friends does she have like that Moncrief creep? Once I get her back home, she's grounded for the next ten years. That's a promise."

Inside the house, time crept past, measured by the slow ticking of the mantel clock. Outside, the sun had set, the sky had clouded over and a slow, steady rain had begun to fall.

Mrs. Gilly, looking as if she'd aged ten years in the past few hours, opened the study door and informed them that Flora had left a casserole before she'd gone home.

The clock, an ornate affair with silver griffins mounted on each side, wheezed and bonged out the hour. It was late. They had called everyone they could think of and were no closer to the truth than ever. Alex had wanted to get in the car and drive, on the grounds that doing anything was better than doing nothing.

Angel reasoned him out of it. He looked sick. He needed to eat, but Angel knew he wouldn't be able to force down a bite. He needed sleep, but she had an idea neither of them would be getting much sleep for the foreseeable future. He was used to being in charge—used to calling the shots, and now, suddenly, he had come up against something he couldn't control, and it was killing him.

"Why?" he exclaimed suddenly. Socking a fist into his palm, he repeated, "Why? Could you just tell me why she thought things were so bad here she had to run away? I told her we'd talk, dammit!"

"And did you?"

He looked as if he were about to cry, and her heart went out to him. But then, her heart had gone out to him so long ago, she figured they were joint owners by now. Not that he knew that. Not that it made any difference. "Alex, do you want me to stay?"

He glanced up, staring at her almost as if he didn't recognize her. That hurt. That hurt almost more than Sandy's being missing. "Yeah, sure—that is, stay if you want to. You know where everything is."

Thank you for your hospitality, she said silently, bitterly. And for the temporary use of your body. And for the brief illusion that you might even love me a little bit.

No one slept. Well—perhaps Mrs. Gilly, and surely Mr. Gilly, who had dealt with the emergency in his usual manner, but Alex didn't even come upstairs to bed. Angel would have heard him. She lay awake in the bed she had used before, staring up at the ceiling, trying to focus on a niggling scrap of memory that kept eluding her. The more she tried to concentrate, the more it shifted out of reach. She'd had a floater in her right eye once, and every time she'd tried to focus on it, it had moved away, just far enough to be distracting—never far enough to be ignored.

The flower beds. She'd been doing the MacDermot job when Sandy had come out to help her that day. Sandy and the boys had hung around the office, drinking Cokes while she was platting it out, and then Sandy had asked if she could try to lay out a flower bed, and she and the boys had gone outside, and later on, Gus had joined them and the boys had gone off to unload the last of the fruit trees, and she'd heard Gus and Sandy laughing outside, and—

Oh, blast, why couldn't she think?

Possibly because the night before, she'd been lying in her own bed, in her own bedroom, with the one man who had fueled her fantasies for as long as she'd been old enough to know what a fantasy was.

At least a fantasy that didn't involve leprechauns or chocolate or pirate treasure.

The eastern sky was just beginning to gray when she slipped out of bed and tiptoed downstairs to the study.

Alex had fallen asleep in his chair. He looked like hell. The bottle of Chivas was still nearly full, and there was an untouched glass on the desk.

"Oh, my sweet baby," Angel murmured. Kurt was supposed to be the responsible one of the old trio—High, Wyde and Handsome. Alex, Gus, and the beautiful, overly serious, overly responsible Kurt.

But Kurt wasn't the only one. Angel had always sensed in Alex a strength of character, a sense of responsibility that had made him seem older than his age, even when he was raising hell after a game, showing off for the cheerleaders, dousing the coach with Gatorade—or drinking too much beer and singing dirty ditties in the back of Kurt's old pickup.

"Wake up, Alex," she whispered, touching him gently on the shoulder. "You're going to get a crick in your neck."

"Oh, um..."

Suddenly, his eyes blinked open and he stared up at her hopefully. "Did she call? Have you heard anything yet?"

"Not yet, but I didn't expect her to call in the middle of the night. We'll hear something in the morning. Come to bed now, Alex. When she calls—" *When, please God—not if.* "You'll need to be fresh and ready to go get her, wherever she is."

"Can't sleep. Need another drink."

He hadn't had more than a few sips, so far as she could tell. "Then finish this one and come upstairs to bed. I'll set the alarm for seven, and you can shower and have breakfast and be ready when we hear."

Angel had an idea where the child was. She intended to call as soon as Alex was asleep again, and if she was right, she was going to kill the pair of them.

But she could kill them later. Right now, Alex needed her.

Eleven

While a pale, lemony dawn struggled through the dismal rain, they stared at each other. Angel had hoped to catch a few minutes' sleep and prayed Alex could do the same. They would need it for what lay ahead.

But when she led him upstairs and left him outside his door, he called after her, "Don't go. Please. I doubt if either one of us can sleep. Maybe if we talk, we can think of something we've missed."

They had already talked until there was nothing else to say, but Angel could no more have denied him than she could have walked to the moon. "Let me borrow something of Sandy's to change into, then." She'd worn her underwear to bed the first time, and then pulled on her clothes before she'd gone downstairs to find him.

Like the rest of the house, his room was elegant but gloomy, with paneled walls and faded Oriental rugs and too much heavy mahogany furniture that looked as if it had been handed down through generations of Hightowers. Dark green chintz draperies were half-closed when she tiptoed through the door, and she opened them to let in the dreary gray light. Was there a law that said the homes of the landed gentry had to resemble mausoleums?

Her own house was an ugly white bungalow built in the forties, rented since then by countless tenants, and currently furnished in late Yard Sale and early Sears Roebuck. But at least it was cheerful.

However, Alex's house was not her problem. Normally at this time of morning, she'd have been sleep-walking through the motions of showering, making breakfast and getting ready to start the day. Instead, a fourteen-and-a-half-year-old girl had deliberately disappeared and now the whole world had tilted on its axis.

Alex was already in bed, shoulders bare, arms crossed under his head. There was something wickedly sensuous about armpits, she thought irrelevantly, with those dark thickets of incredibly soft hair.

Down, girl. This is no time for hanky-panky!

As he continued to watch her, his silvery eyes now pewter dark, she was suddenly overcome by a feeling of unexpected shyness.

She was going to sleep with him again. Or at least, lie with him, which might or might not be a euphemism for something more.

Under the circumstances, she ought to be ashamed of herself for the salacious thoughts that were rapidly filling up her head, never mind her body. Alex's daughter had run away from home. He had come to her for help, and all she could think of was crawling into that monstrous ancestral bed and making mad, passionate love to his body until neither one of them could think of anything else.

She was a terrible person.

Schooling her voice to hide her own gnawing concern, she said, "Alex, Sandy's all right. I feel it in my bones. She has a lot more sense than you give her credit for, and besides, she told you she was with a friend."

She hesitated beside the dark green leather covered chair, a match for the one in his study, then braced herself to climb into bed with him as if it were no big deal. The sheets were cool and silky. His body was a furnace. Angel lay stiffly on her back, crossed her arms over her chest and tried not to look self-conscious.

"I know, I know. It's not as if she'd disappeared off the face of the earth without leaving a trace. She obviously left under her own power, but God, Angel, she's just a baby! There are dangers out there she can't even begin to understand!"

They both fell quiet then as imagination overtook common sense. Alex swore. Angel vowed silently that the minute she got her hands on Miss Alexandra Hightower, she was going to give that child a no-holds barred lecture about responsibility and taking care not to hurt the people who loved her.

Alex swore again. When he reached out to her, Angel could no more have resisted him than steel could resist a magnet. Physically they fit together like hand

and glove. Emotionally, she'd always known it, even when every shred of intellect she possessed said otherwise.

She patted his shoulder and murmured incoherent words of comfort. He stroked her back through a layer of soft cotton knit and echoed her soothing sounds. Angel wasn't sure just who was comforting whom, but she did know that his jaw had that same granitelike look she had seen only once before, when his father had been killed by a drunk driver after a Duke-State game.

"She's *got* to be all right," he growled. "I want to tear down the whole damned world stick by stick until I find her, only I don't know where to start!"

She could sense the rage and the hurt inside him. He was a warrior without a battle, a knight without a dragon to slay.

"I just wish to God she'd chosen some other way to make her point," he muttered.

"Mmm. I was going to ask you about that," Angel said in an effort to distract him. "Do you happen to know what she meant when she said—that is, in her note she mentioned—"

"Us? You and me?" The timbre of his voice, deepened and roughened by stress, rumbled along her spine, setting off all sorts of interesting harmonics in odd parts of her body.

Oh, for pity's sake, here she was all hot and bothered at a time when the last thing on any man's mind would be sex! *Think about work, Angeline. Think compost, think mulch, think—think anything but what you're thinking!*

Trying her darnedest to sound brisk and business-like, she said, "In her note, she mentioned giving us some privacy to work things out. She said you'd know what she meant. Do you?"

While she waited for his reply, her toes curled nervously against his shin. The hair on his legs was surprisingly dark. All his body hair was dark. For a man who was always the epitome of understated elegance in his tweeds, his dark gray pinstripes and even his well-bred casuals, he was shockingly sexy in nothing at all. A fact which, at a time like this, she should be shot for even noticing.

"She knows I went to see you tonight—last night. Whenever the hell it was."

Angel knew precisely to the minute when it was. It was burned on her soul indelibly.

"When I got home, she asked me if—"

"If?" she prompted when he fell silent.

"Nothing," he said, but she had a feeling it was a lot more than merely nothing. She was beginning to suspect it might have more than a little to do with Sandy's running away.

"I thought she liked me," she whispered. Her eyes burned, a result, she told herself, of too little sleep. Alex's arms tightened around her, making her acutely aware of the fact that the only thing between them was a bit of cotton knit in the form of an oversize Wolfpack T-shirt and whatever he wore to sleep in. Which evidently wasn't pajamas, and might not even be briefs. She hadn't dared allow her hands to stray anywhere near the equator.

And she wasn't crying, honestly she wasn't, because Angel never cried, only she must have made some sound because Alex leaned away and stared down at the top of her head, then shoved his fist gently under her chin, lifting her face. "Angel? What is it? Is it something I said?"

He sounded so concerned, she was suddenly furious with him. Furious with Sandy for putting them through this, furious with Alex for sweeping her back into his life, and furious with herself for still caring. "No, dammit, it's not something you said! I happen to be tired and sleepy and—and frantic with worry, and so are you, and if that child doesn't march herself back home in time for breakfast, I—I—"

She gave up. Her face crumpled. Angel hadn't cried since her mother died. She hadn't cried when her husband had been killed. She hadn't cried when she'd found out that the wretch didn't know the meaning of fidelity. She hadn't even cried when her whole house had nearly burned down, but there was a limit, dammit, to just how stoic any woman could be!

Gulping, sniffling and hiccuping, she told him so, and he tucked her head under his chin and resumed stroking her back while he murmured words that were probably meant to be soothing but had the opposite effect, with the flat of his hand burning a hole in her borrowed sleepwear.

"I'm the one who's supposed to b-be comforting you," she said with a watery chuckle.

"Right. Why else would I invite you into my bed?"

As a joke, it fell flat. As a reminder that they were lying entwined in each other's arms in a bed, in the privacy of his bedroom, the effect was electrifying.

"Angel?" Alex whispered.

Acutely attuned to every nuance of his voice, to every inch of his lean, hard body, she was blisteringly aware of the subtle changes in both. A moment ago his voice had been rough with worry and exhaustion. Now it was rough with something else altogether. They had both been unable to relax, but now his tension radiated a different kind of energy.

"Yes," she said simply, meaning everything. Yes, she wanted him. Yes, her heart ached for him because he was frightened and worried and so was she.

Yes, she loved him. Not that he had ever asked for her love. Nor was he asking now, but if for a little while she could offer the comfort of her body—a momentary surcease, no matter how brief—she wouldn't ask for anything in return. "Yes," she whispered, letting her hands play down over his chest.

When her fingertips found his hard nipples he caught his breath, so she kissed him there, swirling her tongue around the tiny button. She felt him leap against her belly and knew a moment of triumph that quickly fled under a deluge of more demanding sensations.

"Ah, sweetheart, yes—please." He groaned, rolling over onto his back, pulling her across his body.

If she had stopped to think about what they were doing, it might have seemed wrong. Knowing that, Angel didn't allow herself to think, only to feel. Stress magnified the urgency of her need and, if the mounting evidence could be believed, of Alex's, as well.

"Take off your shirt," he rasped. He was panting as if he'd just run a three-minute mile.

Tearing herself from his arms was agony, but she sat up in bed, in the dim gray light spilling through the windows, and tugged the stretchy garment over her head. Once free, she flung it to the floor and then cast a shy, sidelong glance down at the man beside her. He was still lying on his back, the sheet tented proudly near his midsection. He was watching her, and she felt her breasts tighten in response. She was already embarrassingly wet, throbbing with need, and he had barely touched her. To her heightened senses, the warm, musky perfume of sex seemed to eddy up around them, an intoxicating counterpoint against the fainter scent of waxed wood and clean linens.

She waited for him to make the first move, and when he didn't, she withered a little. Surely he wasn't waiting for her to take the initiative. She didn't know how. Cal had always hated it when she approached him, and she'd quickly learned to let him take the lead.

Almost as if he'd read her thoughts, Alex said, "Come down here and kiss me." If she didn't know better, she could have sworn there was the echo of a smile in his voice.

As desperately as he needed her mouth, needed her body—needed her in every way there was to need a woman—Alex was almost reluctant to begin, knowing that it would inevitably end too soon. The fuse had been burning too long. Since the first time he'd seen her backing out from under that magnolia tree. Since long before that, if the truth were known.

Crazy as it seemed, nothing that had happened since had lessened that need.

Nor, it occurred to him, had making love with Angel left him feeling depressed and empty. Not that he'd had much time to examine his feelings in the past twenty-four hours.

Slowly, tentatively, Angel lowered her mouth to his, parting her lips and tilting her head to one side. His brittle control slipped another notch. Capturing her mouth, he turned her onto her back and moved over her, careful not to break contact. He was fiercely, achingly aroused, trembling with the need to bury himself inside her small, hot body before he lost what little control he still possessed. She was close to the edge, but he wanted her on the very precipice. It was vitally important to him for reasons he didn't dwell on that she be with him every step of the way. No woman deserved to be left on the ground when she was capable of flying, and Angel flew. Goodness, how she flew!

Without lifting his mouth from hers, he slid one hand down between their heated bodies and found her, found the nest of soft curls, pictured their fiery color, felt the telling moisture and groaned aloud.

Yes, oh, yes! he thought distractedly when her hips lifted to meet his hand. Gently he stroked her, heard her breathing grow shallow and rapid as he brought her closer to the edge. He still couldn't get over how responsive—how generously, tempestuously responsive—she was.

"Alex, I need you," she panted, grinding her hips against his hand, against him. "Now!"

With his free hand, he parted her thighs wide enough to make a place for himself between them. He came into her in one powerful thrust, and then forced himself to wait. She moved against him, agitated, wildly uncontrolled, but he gripped her hips with one hand, forcing her to slow down until he regained his own control.

"Wait," he gasped, but it was already too late. While he was desperately trying to hang on, she was pushing him over the edge, twisting hotly beneath him, raking her teeth over his nipple. "Reckless woman," he panted, a taut parody of a smile twisting his flushed features. "You don't know how dangerously you're living."

Either that or her hunger matched his own, which was too much to hope for. It had been his experience that women were slower to kindle, if they kindled at all. For reasons he didn't take time to explore, it was vitally important that he bring this woman to the ultimate pleasure.

Then she dug her heels into his ribs. Alex grasped her ankles and shoved them up over his shoulders. He rode her hard and fast as she began to convulse around him. "Angel!" he cried. He bared his teeth in a grimace just as her husky cries of release cascaded over him. He stiffened. His body jerked once, twice, and then he shuddered and collapsed.

Eventually he rolled over, carrying her with him, but still he held her, held her as if he would never let her go.

It was raining hard when Angel roused to the distant sound of kitchen noises. She was disappointed, but not really surprised, to find herself alone. Someone, either Alex or Mrs. Gilly, was making breakfast.

She would give her entire fortune to be able to crawl back into her cocoon again, but the world refused to go away. Sandy was still missing. And there was still Alex.

Oh, blast, she had really gone and done it this time.

Stiffly she sat up and shoved her hair from her face, squinting at the clock on the marble-topped dresser across the room. Here the morning was already half-gone, and nothing had been accomplished.

Was that coffee she smelled? Rich, dark and fragrant, it suddenly seemed the most desirable thing in the world. But first she needed to soak the soreness from her body.

No. First there was a call she had to make.

She was still struggling with her priorities a moment later when Alex elbowed open the door. The tray in his hands tilted dangerously as he stared across the gloomy old room filled with the furniture that had belonged to his parents and his grandparents.

Dina had hated it, the way she had hated everything about the house. He had encouraged her to change whatever she wished to change, but she'd never gotten around to it. He knew now it had never been important enough to her.

In Dina's place, Angel would have turned his whole life upside down within six months. Without even trying, she lit up the darkness, brought out the sun, lifted his spirits in a way that should have been impossible, all things considered.

But then, that was Angel. There'd always been something almost luminous about her. Even as a kid she'd had a way of making him feel good, with her forthright honesty and her irrepressible cheerfulness. He had always liked her, but once he started noticing her the way a randy kid noticed girls, he'd tried to keep a certain distance between them.

And then he'd met Dina. The old trio had started to come unglued, and Angel had suddenly dropped out of sight, busy with her own life, according to Gus.

Now here she was, sitting up in his bed with the rumpled bedclothes tucked under her arms, her elbows propped on her bent knees, chin resting in her hands. The same forthright, luminous Angel. She looked so damned delectable it was all he could do not to crawl in with her and seek forgetfulness in her arms again.

"I thought you could start with coffee and toast and then we could have something more substantial," he said.

"Alex, have you talked to any of Sandy's teachers? That Mrs. Toad—"

"Todd."

"Whatever. Anyway, she just might know something that would help."

"Angel, I don't want you to leave."

She gave him a puzzled look. "Then I thought I'd call Gus and see if—"

"Ever."

"Alex, are we talking at cross-purposes here? Look, I think there's a pretty good chance that—"

"Did you hear what I said?"

"You said—*what did you say?*"

Endangering lamp and telephone, he slid the tray onto the bedside table and sat down on the bed beside her. "Listen, I know this is lousy timing, but if we wait, we might get caught up in something else, and I can't take the chance of losing you for another ten or twenty years."

Angel was amazed to see that his hands were unsteady. There were shadows dark as grape jelly under his eyes, and he'd cut himself shaving, and she loved him until she thought her heart would burst, she really did.

Only he was right. This was not the time. "Alex, listen to me carefully. The other day when Sandy was helping me out at the farm and Gus was doing something with my plugs, she started asking about where his house was, and who lived with him, and if I'd ever visited him there."

Evidently she'd caught his attention. Reaching past him, she poured two cups of coffee and fixed his the way he liked it. "So I thought," she said, stirring in just the right amount of sugar, "I thought there might be a chance—"

"In that case, Gus would've called by now, wouldn't he?"

"It depends on how long it took her to get there. If she caught a ride with a friend, then it wouldn't take all that long. A few hours. But if she had to go by bus, it could take a lot longer. Longer still to get from a bus station to his house. And then, if she could convince him that we might—that is, in the stress of the moment, we might possibly—"

"Find out we couldn't live without each other?"

Angel felt her face grow warm. Oh great. This was just what she needed. Her hair looked like a stork's nest, she probably had hickeys all over her neck, and when she was embarrassed, like now, she turned red as a raspberry.

Alex tucked a wild wisp of hair behind her ear, then took another and twisted it around his finger. His eyes had gone from pewter to silver again. "Did I tell you that when I came home from your place, she was waiting for me? She wanted to know if we'd slept together and if I was going to marry you, and why I hadn't brought you home with me. Which, I'm beginning to believe, just might be the whole idea behind this crazy disappearance."

Angel pressed her hands against her burning cheeks. "So now I know, right?"

"Now you know what? That she's with Gus? I'm two jumps ahead of you. I tried to call his house first thing this morning, but there was no answer."

"Did you try his cellular?"

He hadn't had to try the cellular. He'd had a call from Gus while he was in the shower, saying that he was on his way down from the mountains with a passenger, and the two of them would be rolling into town in about an hour.

"Call him. The number's in my purse." That wasn't what she'd meant, however. She'd meant that now she knew why he'd sort of proposed to her...if you could call it a proposal. She would rather he hadn't bothered if all he wanted was someone to help him cope with a teenage daughter.

The distant sound of a car door reached them through the drone of rain on a slate roof. "Flora," said Angel.

"I don't think so." Alex grinned. That solid thud had come from something a lot more substantial than his cook's little Honda. It sounded more like a heavy-duty pickup truck. Offhand, he could think of only one such truck that would be pulling up to his front door at this particular time, and it wasn't the power company's meter reader.

Turning to the disheveled woman in his bed, he leaned over and braced a hand on each side of her thighs, pinning her tightly in place with the covers. "We've got maybe two minutes before they both come barging in on us. Now...do we strike a bargain before your brother and my daughter demand satisfaction, or are you going to watch the pair of them mop up the floor with my bleeding body?"

Angel eyed him suspiciously. "Have you by any chance had a drink this morning?"

Then of course, Alex had to tell her the whole story. By the time he finished, they could hear the clump of Gus's boots on the carpeted stairs, along with Sandy's excited chatter.

"Quickly now—tell me," he demanded. His eyes were laughing, and Angel couldn't remember the last time she'd seen that happen. "Shall I lock the door and have another go at convincing you?"

"This is absurd," she said breathlessly, trying to sound indignant and failing miserably.

"Daddy, are you in there?"

"Last chance," he said softly. "I'm not sure how convincing I can be with a couple of barbarians pounding on the door, but I'm willing to give it my best shot."

"I haven't the slightest idea what you're talking about. Alex, I've never seen you like this before!"

"I've never felt like this before."

"Dammit, Hightower, if you've got my sister in there, you're in deep trouble!" Gus roared through the walnut-paneled door.

"Go away, Wydowski!" Alex called over his shoulder. Leaning closer, he whispered, "Will you?"

"Will I what?" Her voice sounded thready and breathless. Angel had her feet planted firmly on the ground—she wasn't about to take anything for granted.

"Will you make my day? Make my life? Be my Angel?"

On the other hand, nothing ventured, nothing gained, she told herself, melting into his embrace just as two sets of fists began pounding on the bedroom door.

* * * * *

COMING NEXT MONTH

#955 WILDCAT—Rebecca Brandewyne

October's *Man of the Month*, wildcatter Morgan McCain, wanted every inch of city slicker Cat Devlin, but there was no way he was going to let her womanly wiles lure love into his hardened heart.

#956 A WOLF IN THE DESERT—BJ James

Men of the Black Watch

Patience O'Hara knew she was in trouble when she felt more than fear for her dangerously handsome kidnapper. What was it about Matthew Winter Sky that had her hoping her rescue would never come?

#957 THE COWBOY TAKES A LADY—Cindy Gerard

One night with irresistible Sara Stewart had rough-and-tough cowboy Tucker Lambert running for cover. Because falling for Sara would mean saying "I do" for this confirmed bachelor!

#958 A WIFE IN TIME—Cathie Linz

Kane Wilder was driving Susannah Hall crazy! But when they were both sent back in time to solve a mystery, Susannah's only chance for survival was to pose as the stubborn man's wife....

#959 THE BACHELOR'S BRIDE—Audra Adams

Marry Reid James? No way! But Rachel Morgan's pregnancy left her no choice but to accept the infuriating man's proposal— even if it was *just* for her baby....

#960 THE ROGUE AND THE RICH GIRL—Christine Pacheco

Premiere

Prim and proper Nicole Jackson was desperate, and hotshot Ace Lawson was the only man who could help her. Now if she could only be sure he would never discover her secret....